SCRAP

A STEEL BONES MOTORCYCLE CLUB ROMANCE

CATE C. WELLS

Cover art and design by Clarise Tan of CT Cover Creations.
Proofreading by Nevada Martinez.
Special thanks to Jean McConnell of The Word Forager, and always, Louisa.

Thanks for reading! Like what you read? Please do me a solid and leave a review.

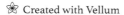 Created with Vellum

1'

CRISTA

Scrap Allenbach is getting out of jail today.

My stupid body's gone haywire. I'm sweating down my back, and my face is so hot, I'm probably as red as a baboon's ass.

Everyone's staring, which doesn't help. After all, I'm the reason Scrap's been upstate for the past ten years.

The Steel Bones clubhouse is crazy, prospects moving furniture to lay out the dance floor, sweetbutts scrubbing down the tables, old ladies banging around in the kitchen. It's not even ten in the morning, and a third keg's already been tapped. It's a huge celebration.

I think I'm gonna puke.

Everyone's acting like they're not watching me blow up balloons. Fay-Lee's been hovering around, all skinny-ass mama hen, as if I'm finally gonna crack and lose my mind. I'm not. I might melt into a puddle of embarrassment right here by the bar, but I'll keep it together. I always —mostly—do.

And as if all the eyeballs weren't enough, Harper Ruth is hovering around.

Harper is Heavy's sister, and Heavy's the president. She sees herself as some kind of Wendy to the Steel Bones' Lost Boys. She's protective, and I get that, but I wish she'd back off. I'm not going to do whatever it is she thinks I'm going to do. She should know that by now. I serve drinks, keep my head down. I'm not going to ruin Scrap's homecoming. Not on purpose, anyway.

Still, she's swinging her lady dick around, making sure I know my place, which is kind of a joke since I've pretty much worn a hole in my place so deep, I couldn't get out if I tried. I hang around in the background, keep the bar stocked, run errands. Try not to ruin any more lives.

"Do you think we need to bring in more pussy?" Harper bares her teeth, her version of a smile, and gauges me with her weird, gray shark eyes.

I keep my head down and press the nozzle on the helium tank. "Sure. Why not?"

I tie off a balloon and hand it to Fay-Lee. This morning, Fay-Lee's in charge of adding the string, and if I'm not mistaken, my mom has asked her to keep an eye on me. Girl's been up my ass all morning.

Harper clicks her fancy pen. "Ten years is a long dry spell. Maybe I should call The White Van, have them close up the place for the night, send all the girls over."

"Sure."

"Okay, then." Harper scrawls on her clipboard with a flourish. "I'll call over now. Unless...." She cocks her head, waiting.

I say nothing and push the button on the tank of air and a bright pink balloon swells up bigger than my head.

Harper keeps going. The woman does not know when to quit. Probably makes her a great lawyer. Definitely makes her an asshole.

"I know a lot of the girls want to give our boy a welcome home he won't forget. If that's gonna be a problem, just—"

My stomach tightens, and the old scars twinge. My whole body is radiating heat. It's a special kind of hell when everyone thinks they know your business, and everyone's got it all wrong.

"It's not like that."

"It isn't?" Harper raises an eyebrow.

I look to Fay-Lee for backup, but she shrugs. I guess that's fair. I don't talk about Scrap. No one really knows what our deal is.

Including me.

But the last thing I want to do right now—or ever—is to talk about it with Harper Ruth. It's hard enough to wrap my brain around the fact that soon, Scrap Allenbach and I are going to be in the same room together for the first time in ten years.

Heavy, my dad, and a few other brothers are picking him up right now. They're taking him to Heavy's cabin for some downtime before they bring him to the clubhouse for the party. The party's supposed to be a surprise. My guess is someone's gonna blow that in the first five minutes.

Scrap's going to be here in a few hours, and we're going to see each other, and then—

Then what?

My stomach flops like a fish on a hook. I fumble the knot I'm trying to tie, and a balloon takes off squealing and farting across the room. Fay-Lee snorts, and a prospect leaps for it, missing and crashing onto a pool table. Brothers howl, all boisterous and day-drunk.

At my feet, my dog Frances harrumphs and rolls over to his other side. Frances is a mostly bloodhound mix who is not now—and has never been—impressed, amused, or interested. He's the freakin' best.

I rub my sweaty palms on my jeans and snag another balloon from the pack.

"I know you and him were never really...?" Harper waits, letting the silence drag out. She should know better. I'm Crista Holt. Master of awkward silences. The walking, talking cautionary tale.

You know how many times I've strolled into a room, and it instantly gets quiet? How many times someone has said something totally innocuous—about Route 12 or Ernestine's hernia surgery or something—and everyone goes mute? Walking in my shoes sucks. My life is like one long cell phone call, interrupted by a series of tunnels.

"The last thing I'd want to do is make this harder..."

Oh, Lord, make it stop. Harper can't really think I'm worried about Scrap Allenbach and a bunch of strippers, can she? What about me says *Back off my man*? I can't even talk to a man I don't know. I can hardly talk to *anyone*.

"Whatever you want to do, Harper."

"But—"

"Last one." I tie off the balloon and hand it to Fay-Lee. "You need anything else?"

Harper narrows her eyes. I stare back, carefully blank.

"No. I guess I've got this handled."

"All right then." I nod at Fay-Lee and bail for the kitchen.

Frances waits until I'm halfway across the room, and then he lumbers to his paws so dramatically and resentfully he should win an Emmy. I swear he's rolling his eyes behind my back. He'll perk up when he realizes where I'm headed. He's a treat whore, and the old ladies spoil him rotten.

Harper's never stepped foot in the kitchen once that I've seen, and I need a break. Besides, based on the number of brothers who've shown this early, I also need to bring more stock up from the back. I filled the shelves last night, but it wouldn't hurt to have a few boxes of extra liquor tucked under the bar. This is looking like the kind of rager that can go two, maybe three days.

My dad Pig Iron is the club treasurer. Technically, he's in charge of the books and the bar. In reality, my mom Deb runs the numbers, and I manage the bar. Dad basically pours drinks for the ladies when he feels like it and keeps his weed in the garnish fridge.

I'm not complaining. It's a good job for me, the clubhouse being one of the few places I know I'm safe, where I'm comfortable. I grew up here, climbing on the tire playset the brothers built in the yard.

When the kitchen doors swing shut behind me and Frances, some of the weight lifts from the stares and the fact that—fuck, fuck, fuckity fuck—Scrap Allenbach's coming home today. It's hot in here, and loud, and it feels like home. My mom's at the industrial stove, messin' around with her girls, Aunt Shirl and Ernestine.

My mom's like this short, round red onion, tucked between Aunt Shirl's skinny carrot and Ernestine's huge, hair-sprayed broccoli head.

"There's my sweet baby!" Ernestine bends to scratch Frances behind the ears.

"Dogs don't belong in a kitchen," my mom mutters, stirring peppers in a cast iron skillet.

"They let Pig Iron in here," Aunt Shirl says and high fives Ernestine who's returned to her place at the stove. Aunt Shirl sniffs Ernestine's pot and then rummages in some jars on the counter.

"You put that bay leaf in my sauce, I'll beat your ass." Ernestine blocks Aunt Shirl with a big wooden spoon.

Aunt Shirl rolls her eyes. "Ain't nobody wanna touch your nasty sauce."

"That's not what Twitch used to say back in the day." Ernestine smirks. She loves bringing up how she used to bang my Uncle Twitch before he met my Aunt Shirl.

Mom snorts. "Ernestine, you still braggin' on dick you bagged during the Nixon administration?"

"Maybe."

"Now what would Grinder think about that?" Aunt Shirl tastes her own sauce and drops the bay leaf back into the jar.

"Now why would I care what that cheatin', no-good, old-ass motherfucker thinks?" Ernestine put Grinder out a few months back. She does it every few years when he goes too far off the chain.

"That's not what you were sayin' when you came by for your binoculars the other day," I say.

I can't help but razz her. Grinder's been stayin' in my spare room for the meanwhile, and it's sad, seeing a man my grandpa's age crying after a woman. Truth be told, I like having him around, though. For safety.

"I needed those binoculars." Ernestine sniffs.

"Bird watching?" Aunt Shirl says "bird watching" like "bullshit."

"Watching that prospect Grinder's got mowin' my lawn." Ernestine shimmies her wide-ass hips, knocking into both Ma and Aunt Shirl 'til they lose their footing. They laugh and shove back.

"Washington or Boom?" Ma asks.

"Boom."

"That prospect could mow my lawn any day." Ma fans herself with a dish towel.

"Ma!"

Ma shrugs. "What? I ain't blind. Or dead."

I wrap my arms around Ma's round middle and rest my chin on her shoulder. She lifts a spoon to my lips. "Taste. It need more salt?"

"Nah. It's good."

"Better than Aunt Shirl's?"

"I'd never say that." Aunt Shirl's thin line of a mouth almost cracks into a smile. Almost.

I love these women. Tough as nails, each one. Aunt Shirl was an emergency room nurse. Back in the day, she did a tour in Vietnam. My Uncle Twitch passed a few years ago, so now she takes care of all the old-timers, making sure they get fed, take their meds. Bikers are hard-living and stubborn as hell, so it's not an easy task.

Ernestine raised four kids, lost one to the crack epidemic, and then she raised three grandkids as her own, and lost another one to opioids a year or two back. So much loss, but whenever they get together, they're just like they are now. Two tall and one wide, hootin' and hollerin', messin' with each other and carrying on.

Survivors.

I wish I was like them.

Most days, I don't feel like a survivor. I feel like a zombie, the leftover pieces of a person who keeps going through sheer momentum and habit, dragged along by other, stronger people. When you live through hell, you're supposed to come out stronger. Like Rambo.

Or like Scrap Allenbach who's comin' home after doing ten years for me. Dad said it himself, so many times during those first months, those first few years. Since Scrap did what he did, I can move on. Make something of myself. Have a life. I don't have to live afraid.

But I do. I have to be afraid every second of the day, I

have no choice, and it's so fucking hard, but I do it. I live like this. I know from the outside, it doesn't look like much, but I dare anyone to keep the secrets I keep, carry what I carry, and do better.

I'm twenty-six years old, and I live above my parent's garage. I tend bar at the MC clubhouse, I run errands to the club's businesses, not the construction sites but the Autowerks or strip club. I go to doctor's appointments. I watch my sister Annie's kids, and I read.

That's the perimeter of my life. Books, the club, the doctor's, home. And sometimes, when I need to look the past in the eye, when the *living with it* gets to be too much and I have the self-destructive urge to tempt fate, I visit the parking lot of Finnegan's Ice Cream Parlor, and I stare at a man at a gas station.

I've pulled it up on a map on the internet. The perimeter of my life makes a wonky hexagon.

Mom buys my groceries when she gets hers from the bulk store near Pyle. I get my books and jeans and hoodies online. In the past ten years, I've never been on a date or a vacation or swimming or shopping or dancing at Sawdust on the Floor.

I know it sounds sad, like I'd have a lot of time on my hands, but it is so hard, so *time consuming* to walk that perimeter, be vigilant, make sure I'm safe and everything is under control.

Now Scrap's coming home, and it doesn't feel safe, and it sure as hell doesn't feel like I have things under control.

The good ol' trembles start, and under my chest, Mom stiffens. She wraps her arms around mine and rocks slowly, foot to foot. "How ya doin' baby?"

Aunt Shirl and Ernestine's faces go grim, and they sway nearer like two tall trees, offering comfort, cover. I let the closeness seep in, let their presence take the weight, again.

"I'm fine."

"No one would blame you if you went home." Ma cranes her neck to meet my eyes.

I roll my eyes. "*Everyone* would blame me."

"You don't owe them anything."

"I owe Scrap." It wasn't my choice, but all the same. I owe him. "Don't I?"

There's a long moment of silence over the stove while around us in the huge kitchen, the banging and chatter goes on.

"It was his decision." Aunt Shirl plunges her spoon into her pot, swirling the thick, red sauce like she means business. "No one asked him to do it."

"Especially not in public like that." Mom sucks the inside of her cheeks. She's never made any bones about the fact she thinks what Scrap did was stupid. It's not a popular opinion around here.

"He'd just lost his parents. And he was so young." Ernestine sounds like the weary grandma. Scrap's not her blood, but she considers all the boys hers, especially those like Scrap who were born into the club.

This is more than people usually say around me. Most of the time, we all sweep what happened out the door when it inevitably shows up. Ignore it like cobwebs up in high corners. That makes it easy for me to keep my secrets, but sometimes, the need to talk about it comes over me like a compulsion.

I get this insatiable, morbid curiosity, a kind of burning itch where I want to scratch at the past, see what's underneath, but talking about it hurts Mom more than me, so I don't ask her. I know I should just be grateful.

I have my dad because Scrap Allenbach did what he did, so my dad didn't have to. So I didn't have to lose anything more than I did on the floor of that gas station. I can never repay him. Not that it matters. He wants nothing from me.

Back when I was first recovering, when the insomnia was so bad I started hallucinating, Mom thought it'd help me to see Scrap. Dad wanted me nowhere near SCI Wayne, but Mom made him take me to visit. She had this idea that seeing him would help, somehow convince my lizard brain that I was safe and let me sleep. It was a fool's errand. I knew I wasn't safe.

Still, Dad drove me the three hours upstate, and I sat behind a thick pane of glass while guards brought in a man I hardly recognized.

Scrap's left eye was swollen shut, his lip was split, and he had a cut on his right temple as if someone started carving the letter L on a slant. I was slammed with guilt. My throat closed, my breathing strangled to a wheeze. I had a panic attack in a staticky, plastic chair while Scrap Allenbach told me he didn't want me there, to never come back.

"Please. I'm so sorry," I'd blubbered, snot running from my nose.

"Not as sorry as I am." He'd stared at a spot over my shoulder, sharp jaw clenched so tight I could see each cord in his neck, his hands fisted in his lap. If I hadn't already been so low, the weight of his words would have crushed me to pieces.

Of course, I never went back. Never asked about him again. Some people in the club think I'm a cold bitch because of it, and I let them. Better than telling them their hero wishes he'd never seen my face.

"Crista? Crista?"

Oh, shit. I drifted off. All three ladies have turned away

from the stove, worrying at me with their sad eyes and their sad smiles. My skin heats with irritation. I need to pull it together. Freaking them out is the last thing I want to do.

I shake it off like I always do, smiling to reassure them that what's broken down in front of their eyes is just fine after all.

I sheepishly shake my head, and press my forehead to Mom's. Then I smack a kiss on Aunt Shirl's cheek and grab the spoon from Ernestine's hand.

"Don't mind me. I'm just spacing out. Now let me try this sauce." I take a taste of Aunt Shirl's and screw up my face. "Too much bay leaf."

Ernestine hoots, and the ladies erupt in shouts and laughter, happy to be distracted, to keep going on as if this is a happy day. There's nothing to see here. I'm not a ghost haunting this place. We're not celebrating the waste of ten years of a man's life. It's all fine.

I'm fine.

Scrap Allenbach is coming home.

When I can get away, Frances and I go down to storage for a few more bottles to stash under the bar, and as soon as I'm away from other people—just like I knew it would—the compulsion hits. I have to check and make sure everything's okay.

If I were home, I'd check the door. The windows. The closets. If I were in my car, I'd check the rearview. The Beretta Nano in the glovebox. Pop it open, take a quick glance, pop it shut. Everything's okay.

I'm at the clubhouse, though, surrounded by family, as protected as I can ever be. Still, the itch crawls up my spine and spreads over my skin. How do you convince yourself that you're safe when you *are* safe, but your body doesn't believe it? I check. Then I check again.

I bend, touch the knife in my ankle sheath. Slide it out, tuck it back in. It helps, but not much. Not enough.

Shit. There's only one way to deal with the urge when it won't go away.

I don't want to. A knot coils in my stomach as my hand reaches into my pocket for my phone. Looking at the photo fucks with my head almost as much as the itch.

Almost.

I shouldn't need to look. What good can it really do? I can't calm myself down, though. Not on my own. Not with lazy 8 breathing or visualization or slamming shots. And if I leave the compulsion to fester, it'll become a panic attack, and the hydroxyzine will put me in bed for the rest of the day. If I take a pass on the pills, I'm rolling the dice that the panic won't put me on the floor and slap a look of pity on everyone's face.

My fingers shake while I swipe the unlock code, F for Frances. I tap my photos. Tap again on a folder with one picture in it, and his face appears, so familiar now that I have to force my eyes to focus on the features: the eyes, the chin. Instantly, the itch is doused by a jolt of adrenaline, a full body slam that sends me sinking to my butt against the wall.

He's in profile. An open hood in the background. His mouth is open, mid-sentence. His face is tan. Healthy. You can only see one blue eye, and the faint outline of the tattoo on his neck.

It's an older picture. He looks different now. Life's been hard.

I should delete it. It does nothing but drag me back. I figured out a long time ago I'm not the kind with the guts to do anything about it myself. If I thought I'd ever move forward, maybe I would delete it. But I'm stuck as sure as

Scrap Allenbach has been for the past ten years, a prisoner of a different kind. He's coming home today, and I never left. I don't know why I spent the morning blowing up balloons.

I shove my phone back in my pocket and grab a box to carry the booze in. Frances turns three times in a circle and flops down, blocking the door. He's snoring before I've pulled a single bottle off the shelf.

He's gonna be a grumpy pup in five minutes when I have to wake him up to leave.

This is a party, after all. I got shit I need to do.

2

SCRAP

The bike's the only thing that feels right.

Shoes with hard soles feel weird. Jeans feel weird. Pickin' shit off a menu feels weird. Do I want the fries or the onion rings? And it's like you gotta know how to work the computer from *Minority Report* to get your drink. There ain't six flavors of pop no more; there's a shit ton. Do I want regular or diet? What kind of fake sugar? They got a whole other kind now. You want vanilla or cherry or lime?

Fuck. I give up, man. I tap the button that says water and sit back down with my brothers. It's weird sittin' down to eat in a chair with a back. Hell, it's weird eatin' without havin' to *watch* your back.

I just wanna see Crista.

The thought lets air flow into my lungs. I bring her to mind, the same picture I always go to, her waitin' for me on the stairs in front of Petty's Mill High. Long hair shinin', mostly brown but reddish when it catches the light, the hem of her sundress flippin' in the breeze, clarinet case clutched in two hands. Her shy smile quirkin' up the corners of her sweet mouth. I know she's older now. With what she's been through...she ain't gonna be the same. I know this.

She's good, though. My brothers keep me updated. Not much. No pics. She don't like havin' her picture taken. Besides, I couldn't handle it, gettin' too clear a picture of her outside when I was locked up, so I never asked, and they never volunteered. But she's done well. Moved out, workin'. Happy.

I bet her tits are bigger now. She was kind of skinny back then, with these little apple-sized titties, but goin' by Deb and Annie, I bet she grew some. Don't matter. She's healthy. Ain't needed surgery in a long time, now. She's good.

Now, me, I'm antsy as hell. Wired. I been that way since the parole hearing. Like my skin's stretched too tight over my muscles. Ain't been sleepin' much. Or eatin'. I kept runnin' every movie through my mind where a cop is on his last day of the job, and he gets shot.

All this week, I been waitin' for a shank in the back or for them to toss my cell and find a bag of cocaine or something. Bang of the gavel. Ten more years. Nothing happened though 'cept some paperwork and some bullshit wait for an asshole to get back from his coffee break to sign some shit.

I thought the shakes would go when I cleared the place, but not even that long ride down here could soothe me. My knee's jiggling, and Creech, who's pulled up to the table beside me, keeps shootin' me irritated looks. He looks the same as he did before. The tattoos on his head are faded, but other than that, he's the same asshole.

"What?" I finally ask.

"You got to piss?"

"You got even freakier since I went in, eh?"

The brothers laugh, and fuck, it hits me in the chest. I'm

back. Home. The agitation eases, turns a little more into anticipation.

"We headin' to the clubhouse after this?" I wasn't hungry, but Heavy's playin' road captain today, and the burger joint was his idea.

I don't want to say straight out *Can't we go see Crista?* Her dad's sittin' right there, and even though we understand each other, I ain't gonna disrespect him. That's what I want, though. Her sweet, shy smile. Her slight weight in my lap like that charmed day before the world went to hell.

Heavy strokes his long-ass beard. When I went in, it had some length, but now it's like the love child of ZZ Top and fuckin' Gandalf. Crazy. "Thought we'd go out to my cabin first. Relax. Open a bottle of Macallan."

I set my cup back on my tray. Take a pause. Try to find words that don't sound ungrateful.

Unless Crista Holt's at his house, naked with that bottle of whiskey, I ain't gonna relax. She needs to be in my arms. Under me. Fillin' my hands. But it ain't like I can say that. Not with her dad watchin' me like he's my own proud papa, ketchup dribblin' down his gray heard. Still, these fuckers are my brothers. How do they not know that I need to be balls deep in my girl?

"I really want to see everyone. Crista." They exchange looks. What the fuck? This can't be a surprise; they must know I want to see her.

"The women are puttin' together a surprise party for you, man." Creech mumbles through the burger he's chewin'. "You gonna ruin the surprise."

Nickel punches him in the arm at the same time Forty reaches across the table and slaps him across the back of the head. Funny how they move. Nickel like a street fighter, and Forty like the soldier he used to be.

"Dumbass," Pig Iron grunts.

"Well. Surprise is ruined. Might as well head to the club-house." I shoot Heavy a look. He's the boss, but end of the day, I ain't got a warden no more. I'm gonna do what I want. And I want to see Crista.

She works the bar at the clubhouse now. I would've thought she'd have some fancy office job with how smart she is and how good she was at school. Maybe even gone to college like Harper and Heavy. But I guess all them surgeries at the beginning got in the way of that. She's happy, though, so who cares, right?

Heavy shakes his head slow. "The women'll be mighty pissed if we ruin all their hard work. Let's go to my place. You can get a shower. Pick your own clothes."

"Yeah, you smell like inmate, man. You gotta wash that off." Creech waves at me with a fry.

"What's inmate smell like?" I take a sniff of my shirt. Don't smell nothin'.

"Public bathroom soap and ball sweat." Charge flashes his pretty-boy smile. He should know. He's done enough time himself.

"Oh, so like your mom?" I grin back.

The table cracks up. More weight lifts. All of a sudden, I want to get back on the road. Not only to get closer to Crista, but because I need that wind in my face again.

"So my place?" Heavy asks.

The need to see Crista wars with the desire to ride off these past years, air out any darkness that still's clinging to me. She's so sweet, so innocent. She don't need to be anywhere near the filth I been wallowin' in these past ten years. I nod, push back my tray.

We're back in the saddle in no time, and as if he's in my head, Heavy takes us by way of the scenic route, picking up the Luckahannock north of Pyle and riding along the river. It's a perfect early spring day. The wind has a bite, and the sun seems far off overhead. The river runs fast and wild, racing at our side.

I ain't never regretted what I done, but damn, I have missed the world.

Sunshine. Open road. Crista Holt. All the proof of God a man could ever need.

As I ride, I throw the doors in my soul open, set all the wanting in me free, let my heart finally feel what it's been dyin' for. In a few hours, Crista will finally be in my arms. I'll wrap that long, silky hair in my fist, toss whatever pretty little dress she's got on up, and drink her shy smiles in while I stroke inside her sweet pussy. Show her I ain't never goin' anywhere ever again.

I ain't stupid. I know it ain't really gonna go down like that. It's been a long time, and when I went away, she was only sixteen, and I'd kept some distance out of respect for her age and for Pig Iron. We shared a few rides and a stolen kiss at a picnic. And then at Wayne, I sent her away. It was the right call at the time, but it's stolen more than one night's sleep from me.

I know she ain't gonna run to me, leap into my arms.

But the dream? Under this blue sky, ridin' beside my brothers...it don't seem so impossible. Not when God can make a day like this.

3

CRISTA

My heart's slamming against my rib cage like a loose shutter in a gale-force wind. The roar of motorcycles pulling up in front of the clubhouse is matched by the roar of the crowd of men inside, echoing off the vaulted roof. Women whoop, feet stomp, and there's a clinking as dozens of bottles are tapped together.

He's here.

I try to swallow, but my throat's too tight. What do I do with my hands? I grab a rag, swipe a condensation ring off the bar. No, that's wrong—disrespectful somehow—so I stop, and snake my hands up into my hoodie sleeves.

There's a mob of people between where I stand and the front, so I can see when the doors swing open, but I can't see the men who walk in. The crowd surges in that direction, and a cry rises and echoes in the renovated arch-roofed garage that serves as bar, game room, and dance hall for the MC.

"Scrap! Scrap! Scrap!"

Sweetbutts clamber up onto tables, flashing their tits, and a prospect pops a bottle of champagne, dousing the knot of men wending their way through the onslaught. Is that Dom? Where the hell did that kid get his hands on that? Damn. I must've left the storage unlocked earlier when I stocked up. Shit. That ain't cheap.

I knead the wristbands of my hoodie, squeezing, dampening the fabric with my palm sweat. I need to calm down. Pull it together.

It's nice that for the first time in weeks, there are no eyes on me. Everyone's either following the slow procession, some old-timers like Boots and Gus with tears in their eyes, or they're elbowing forward to clasp hands and slap backs. From my position behind the bar on the far wall, all I catch are glimpses.

Heavy, all huge and hairy, stands to the side for once, accepting the overflow of congratulations like a benevolent giant. Nickel's scowling, and Charge is charming his way through the press of drunken, messy bikers and hang-arounds, old ladies and club pussy. My dad brings up the rear of the entourage, chest swelled with pride as if this is his son and a truly happy day, not the postscript to a tragedy.

And there—in the middle—Scrap. The air whooshes from my lungs, and in my sleeves, my hands fist, my nails biting into my palms.

Damn. He's so much *older*.

His hair's buzzed like it was the last time I saw him, ten years ago behind that thick pane of glass at SCI Wayne. He's filled out in the shoulders, imposing even next to Forty and Charge, but he's still cut more like Nickel, less thick and burly, more chiseled and hard.

My cheeks heat and my heart kicks up a notch. I don't recognize the feeling, half panic, half fascination.

A brother raises a beer, shouts a toast, and Scrap's lips

curve in a half-smile—oh, I *remember* that smile. It's the same smile—kind of wry, kind of chagrined—and the past rushes over me in a cold gust, goosebumps prickling my arms and the back of my neck.

He smiled like that the handful of times when my dad had him pick me up from band practice on his bobber. He'd carefully tuck my clarinet in his saddlebag while I flushed so hot, with all the other band kids gawking from the steps of Petty's Mill High, I thought I'd burn up on the spot. He'd hand me a turtle shell, smiling that smile, and I couldn't look him in the eye for weeks afterwards. Months.

He'd smiled that way before he kissed me that day out back by the firepit. That quick brush of lips. Still my only kiss. My stomach does something weird and squishy. I ignore it before my face flames even worse than it is now.

Scrap's talking to Harper now. He stands still and steady, the way men do who are taller than most. I can make out a scar on his temple and faint lines dusting the corner of his eyes. In my memory, he's twenty-one, but this is a grown man making his way across the clubhouse, each step closer to me. My heartbeat ratchets up another notch.

I need to get busy. Pour some drinks. I scan for empties, but...nothing. My gaze darts left and right. There's no one at the bar. Oh, ugh. This is no accident. The bar's always two or three deep when we have crowds like tonight, but there's no one on the stools, no one standing anywhere near.

It's a setup. My mom's hovering from a distance, leaning in the doorway to the kitchen, my sister Annie next to her. Heavy's escorting Scrap this way, and everyone's made themselves scarce. God, this is so embarrassing. What do they think? We're gonna run into each other's arms like the last scene of *Dirty Dancing*?

I bet they do think that. That's the story, after all. He's

the white knight; I'm the damsel in distress. Sweat breaks out under my boobs and behind my knees. I wipe my palms on my baggy jeans.

I am so not dressed the part of the princess. Although I didn't ask them to, Mom and Annie went to the mall and bought me a dress for tonight. It was the kind I used to wear, a swingy skirt with a tiny print, the outline of birds and foxes made to look like flowers from a distance.

It was so pretty. I tried it on, the first time I'd worn a dress in as long as I can remember. Then, I stood in front of the mirror for ten minutes, staring at all the places the seams strained. It was stretched taut across my boobs and my doughy middle. The hem of the sleeves dug into my jiggly upper arms. My skin was so white against the fabric it looked almost blue, and my big thighs smooshed together unless I move my feet so far apart it looks like I was about to do squats.

Welcome back, Scrap. Remember me? I ate the girl you used to know.

It never felt so good to pull on my jeans and hoodie.

Anyway, if the crowd's expecting an "I've had the time of my life" lift, it ain't happening. For so many reasons.

The men are getting real close now, and Scrap's so tall I can see him survey the room, despite the cluster surrounding him.

Is he looking for me?

Shivers shoot down my spine.

Ten years ago, when Scrap sent me away, Dad tried to explain during the ride home. When a man is looking at hard time, he has to do what he has to do to make it. Sometimes he pushes people away. I knew that was bullshit, but I didn't say anything. Dad felt guilty enough that Scrap was the one to end Inch Johnson. I didn't need to add to the guilt by letting Dad know that Scrap regretted doing it.

Everyone in the club thinks Scrap's carrying this huge torch for me, but he's not. I know he didn't really mean to do what he did. Not kill a man. Scrap probably wishes I'd get gone, let him have a fresh start without a human reminder of the mistake that cost him a decade of his life.

Everyone acts like I know him, but I don't. I was a kid back then. All I remember are snatches. A few rides on the back of his bike after band practice. Playing cornhole at a picnic. The kiss. The weight of his body on my torso while my guts leaked out on a concrete floor.

God, I don't know what to do.

What do you do when the man who held in your intestines so you didn't die finally comes home from jail?

I reach under the bar, grab some limes and a knife. I slice one down the middle, managing to crush half in the process. Damn. I shake out my hands, refocus. I salvage what I can and grab another, but I can't stop glancing up, checking Scrap's slow progress, and now I'm making a huge mess. There's juice and pulp everywhere. I nearly nick my thumb.

And then he's there. A few feet away. I look up, and he's staring at me. All the blood in my body floods to my feet, leaving my heart sputtering in a void, and I sway into the bar, praying I don't crumple to the floor.

He keeps staring. Why is he staring? His face is a careful blank, his faded blue eyes burning. With what? My anxiety ratchets up another notch, and how high can it possibly get before my chest just explodes?

He hates me. That burning look is hate and regret that a dumbass thing he did when he was barely drinking age, trying to be a hero, cost him his entire twenties. Maybe he hates himself.

God, he must wish that I wasn't here. I know the feeling; there's no part of me that wants to be here now, the star of some sick and twisted reality show.

I duck my eyes, focusing on the limes, absolving him of any obligation to speak to me, wishing hard as hell that he lets himself be carried off by the crowd of well-wishers.

Since I've got my head down, I don't see him close the distance between us, but I can feel his presence like a drop in the barometric pressure. My head starts pounding in tandem with my heart, and my hands shake. Then his hands are over mine, quick and steady, and he takes the knife, setting it across the corner of the cutting board.

"You gonna lose a finger." His voice is low, and it's careful, too. Like he's hiding something.

I swallow and my gaze darts up, dragged by some kind of compulsion, even though I'm sweating bullets, and all I want to do is run and hide. I feel so wrong. So big and awkward-shaped and gross.

I force myself to say it. "Hi, Scrap."

"Hi."

There's a bar between us, and he's giving me space, a foot or so, but he's still too close. And it's not just him, he's brought company, flashes of sights and smells that burst into the periphery of my awareness and recede, burning me like embers flung from a fire. *Gasoline and piss. Cold concrete. Copper. Muted sunshine through clouded, yellowed glass.*

I whimper low in my throat, and Scrap's whole demeanor changes. He straightens, his stance widening. Those blank, blue eyes darken and grow wary.

"Hey now...." It's what a movie cowboy says to a skittish horse.

I'm flustered, unsteady on my feet, and I don't know what to do, what to say. I fumble for a plastic tub and drop the lime wedges in.

He stands there. Waiting.

Everyone around us is standing there, waiting.

What does he want? I've got nothing.

He clears his throat. "Can I have a beer?"

Oh. Fuck. My gaze flies up.

His lips curve. Bemused. Distracting.

"Oh. Sorry. Yeah." I blink, searching, as if this isn't my job, and I don't know where everything is. "Do you want a draft?"

"Bottle's fine."

"Bud?"

"That'd be fine."

I grab one, slide it to him, my fingers working on muscle memory, which is a good thing 'cause I can't stop alternating between taking him in and desperately staring at anything else. The initial shock is gone, the memories shoved back down, and I'm overwhelmed and embarrassed and, strangely, completely...fascinated.

He's so *tall*.

He's still standing, and the bar that hits me above the waist hardly comes up past his hips. He's wearing brand new jeans and a gray T-shirt with the Steel Bones Construction logo on the breast. The shirt's tight, especially where his biceps and pecs strain at the fabric. My breath shallows. Shit. Am I panicking? No. This isn't panic. This is...I don't even know.

I sneak a glance up at Scrap again. He was always tall and built, but now he dominates the space, and he's ripped, with the body of a boxer. An athlete. He's honed, even more than Forty who spends hours at the gym every day.

A sick feeling roils my stomach. Oh, fuck. He's ripped because he's had nothing else to do with his days except workout. Not this whole time while I've been eating my feelings and hiding in my e-reader—

I force down the wave of guilt, search for something to say. Come up with nothing.

"You cut your hair." His voice gives nothing away, but still when I look up, his gaze hits me, socks me right in the gut. Now I can see what those carefully blank eyes were hiding. Oh, fuck. Why didn't I recognize it off the bat? I should have; it's not like I don't see it all day, every day.

Scrap Allenbach doesn't feel hate or regret. That's pity in his eyes. Disappointment. Disgust.

My heart sinks. My fingers fly up to my short bob, drop again. I used to have hair down to my butt. After the attack, they had to shave part to stitch the gash in my head, and when Mom "evened it out" in rehab, she made such a mess, it was easier to chop it all off. Now, I keep it short so I don't look like I used to. For safety.

Back when I visited Scrap upstate, I was wearing hats twenty-four/seven. He must remember my hair long and wavy. And me thin and pretty and sixteen. He must remember—

Scrap pressing down on my chest, pinning me hard to the floor, staunching the blood with his body, Dad cupping my cheek, crying. Men shouting. Gasoline and piss. Concrete. Yellowed glass.

My brain glitches, a lightning bolt blinding and deafening me with a crack that sends my body into overdrive as the past plows into the present. I brace for impact, forcing my body to stay in place, stay upright. I'm an old pro at this. I can ride a flashback like a killer wave.

"Why'd you cut your hair?" Scrap can't tell he's talking to a rip in time.

I fight back, shove at the memories so hard, drag in a desperate breath. Why did I cut my hair? Is that what he wants to know?

I have to answer, but I'm having trouble calling up words, there's too much shit loose and ricocheting in my brain.

Scrap's sweeping me with his gaze, and the pity and the disappointment is so damn obvious now, my skin crawls. He notices me bracing and pulling myself back together. And now he's taking in my ratty old hoodie, holes worn in the cuffs so I can slip my thumbs through, my baggy jeans, my scuffed boots.

I know I dress butch. I have my reasons. And nobody cares or even notices anymore—not even Dad—but Scrap Allenbach looks at me like I'm wrong somehow. Like I've offended his fashion sense.

Yeah, I'm fucking wrong. I'm not the sixteen-year-old band geek he crushed on anymore, the girl who painted her toes and wore sandals almost year-round, who braided her long hair for the ride home on the back of his bobber.

I haven't been her in ten years. If he'd been around, he'd know. If he hadn't told me to leave and never come back that day at SCI Wayne, he'd know.

"Why is it your business?" There's anger in my voice. Where did that come from? That's not me, but I can't tamp it down. Not when he's looking at me like I somehow let him down while a tornado swirls inside me, trying to suck me up into the past.

Scrap lowers his beer and rests his hands, calmly, deliberately, on the bar. His blue eyes heat—is he angry, too?— and his Adam's apple bobs as he swallows, all deadly serious.

"Crista." He says my name soft, but there's criticism in it, a chiding, and I don't know what he wants.

My chest squeezes. The more I cast around for something to say, the more lost I feel.

"What? What do you want from me?" Again, there's an uncharacteristic harshness in my voice, and I don't mean it, but from the corner of my eye, I see that Harper and Heavy overhear. Heavy grimaces, and Harper snarls.

"Nothin', babe. I didn't mean to upset you." Scrap drums his fingers a few times on the bar, and then he grabs his beer. "Guess I'll leave you be."

I nod.

He waits a second.

I open my mouth, but nothing comes out.

He turns and walks away.

4

CRISTA

As Scrap stalks off, I nod 'cause that's all I can do. I grab another lime, but my hands are stupid. I can't think of what to do. I end up staring at the cutting board like an idiot.

Mom starts asking for drink orders, and Annie grabs my hand, and I follow her, numb, down the corridor to the annex. On the way, I overhear some sweetbutts too drunk to whisper.

"Do you think she's losing it?"

"Nah. When she's about to lose it, she gets all spastic."

"Shit, a man does that for you...You kind of think she could have pulled it together, welcome him home right, you know?"

My gut clenches. I stop in my tracks, but Annie yanks me forward.

I hear, "She's just totally fucked up. Wouldn't you be? I mean, damn. Poor woman." And then one of them notices me and shushes the others.

"Ignore it," Annie hisses, shooting them the look of death, and leads me off to Mom's office at the end of the hall.

She drags me inside, shoves me toward Mom's desk chair, and then she goes rooting around in Mom's desk.

I stand there, seething. I hate pity. People can say what they want, think what they want, but they can shove their pity up their asses. No one knows what it takes to live like this. They think we're safe, and they have no idea that safety is never anything but an illusion.

God, I wish I hadn't taken Frances home earlier. Frances understands. He's seen me hyperventilate at the front door. Walk through it anyway and force myself to the car, step by step, open the door, key in the lock, buckle up, put it in reverse, all while forcing breath in and out, sweating bullets, and fighting the terror shakes. Frances has seen it all, and he just rolls his eyes.

That's the appropriate reaction. Don't pity me. I'm not in bed. I'm not in the ground. I'm not letting one more person suffer for me. Every goddamn day is a victory.

Annie slams a drawer shut and opens another. In her tight black dress with her fake tits hanging out, she looks like a hooker robbing the place. What the hell is she doing?

"Annie?"

Annie holds up a finger. "Wait for it." She shuffles some papers around, and then she pops up, a joint in one hand and a little orange bottle in the other.

"Good ol' Deb." My older sister hoists up her finds in victory. "You want a happy pill, a toke, or both?"

I make myself sit, purposefully unclench my fists.

"I'm good. I'm fine."

There's the scrape and hiss of a Bic. The smell of some truly dank weed fills the air, and Annie starts hacking up a lung.

It takes her a good few minutes to wheeze out, "Deb is so retro. Who even rolls joints anymore?"

"You know that's probably been in there since 1995." I lean back, let all the stress of the past twenty minutes go.

"Nah." Annie grins. "I smoked all her nineties weed when I was in high school. Somebody's definitely had to re-up the old gal in the past few years."

"Who do you think her hook up is?" This is good. Dumb, distracting conversation.

"Definitely Dad."

"You think?"

"Nobody wants a mellow Deb more than Dad does."

Now that's the truth. Mom is crazy smart and capable— if she were working at a real company instead of Steel Bones, she'd have a corner office—but she's high strung. A pang of guilt messes with my hard-won equilibrium. Mom's anxiety probably has a lot to do with what happened to me. The orange bottles didn't show up until after.

Annie shoves aside a stack of files and sinks onto Ma's sofa, spinning me in the chair so I face her.

"You freaking out?"

I shake my head. "I'm good."

"So was it everything you dreamed it'd be?" Annie takes another drag, smacks her red, matte lips, and blows smoke rings in my face.

"Pretty much." I fan my hand. Shit reeks of skunk. "Are you gonna go home to the kids tonight all buzzed?"

"Of course not. I'm the good parent, remember? I got a babysitter. I'm crashing right here tonight."

I raise an eyebrow. I've been so consumed by my own drama, I didn't really think about how this club reunion is gonna rock a lot of boats.

"Bullet's been bunking here, hasn't he?"

Annie's face goes defensive. "Yup." She draws the

syllable out until you can hear *that deadbeat asshole* in it. Also the *I'm gonna fuck him anyway for shits and giggles*.

"You want to get him naked and seduce him while I steal his wallet?" I waggle my eyebrows.

Annie throws her head back and cracks up. It's so funny 'cause we've done it before. Twice. It was a bust both times. Dude has dust bunnies in his wallet.

"Goddamn Bullet Nowicki." My sister sinks back into the sofa, tucking her knobby knees to her chin.

"All cock, no brains."

"Big dick, small bank account."

"Great lay, bad choice?"

Annie shrugs. "I don't know about that. The man makes beautiful babies."

That he does. My three nieces are perfect blonde-haired, blue-eyed children of the devil.

"He loves those girls to pieces." I say the thing I always say.

It's the truth, but it doesn't make much of a difference. If Mom didn't garnish Bullet's dividend from Steel Bones Construction, Annie's ex would be nine years in arrears for child support. He basically lives at the OTB. He's addicted to the races and poker—and the lotto, probably—and he's unlucky to boot.

"Almost as much as he loves the ponies." Annie sighs, and then she kicks off her high heels and wiggles her toes. They are so long and so gross.

"Quit wavin' those creepy foot-fingers at me." I lean back again, cracking my spine. For the first time in weeks, I start to feel okay, here in this dim office, hiding out with my big sister. The good thing about having Annie Holt for a big sister—she's kind of a human no-judgement zone. Whatever you did, she did worse, and she knew better when she did it.

"So what did he say?"

"He asked for a beer. And he wanted to know why I cut my hair."

"Why's that his fuckin' business?"

"Exactly what I said."

"You do need to stop having Mom cut it. You look like John Cusack." Annie squints at me, her blue eyes puffy slits.

"Do not."

"Do too." Annie's snickering, and she must not smoke-up that much anymore, 'cause the snickering sets her to coughing.

"*Say Anything* John Cusack or *High Fidelity* John Cusack?"

"*High Fidelity*. You've got those sad, loser bangs."

"It's 'cause I'm a sad loser."

"True, true." Annie shakes her head sadly. "It's not your fault. You were born that way."

I kick at Annie's long legs, but I miss, hit the couch, and roll a few inches back. My chest truly eases for the first time in days. It feels so good to take a deep breath.

"Oh, Annie. It was horrible." I squeeze my eyes shut.

"It looked awkward as hell."

"You were watching?"

"Honey, we were *all* watching. It was like the *Bachelor* over there. The biker version of the rose ceremony."

"Must have been disappointing."

"It would've been if I hadn't betted on painful silence and awkwardness. As it was, I should have doubled-the-fuck *down*."

"You always have my back, don't you?"

She winks. "You know I do."

"Everyone hates me now, don't they?" Before he did what he did, Scrap was the low-key, stand-up brother everyone loved. Since he went away, he's become a legend. A saint, more or less. And I'm the poor, broken bitch who doesn't ever visit him. Or talk about him.

Annie extends her legs, propping them on my lap, and yawns. She's always been a lightweight. A few tokes, and her filter's gone. A few more, and she'll be out like a light.

"Nobody hates you. You're the victim, remember?" Yeah, she's definitely past the point of thinking very hard about what she's saying. "I mean, *survivor*."

"You say that like it's not a good thing."

Annie sighs, a loud, inebriated bellow. "It's hard being the fuck-up when your sister's..."

"Perfect?"

Annie snorts. "A perfect bitch."

"I love you, big sister."

"I don't know why." Annie sighs and picks at the paint on her nails.

"'Cause you're the only one who's real with me."

"Seriously?" Annie's eyes go shiny. Oh, shit. She's going to cry. I hate maudlin Annie.

"Yeah. A real bitch." I grin, and she shrieks, digging her toes into my belly, and I slap at her feet, and we laugh until I slip off Mom's ergonomic chair and fall flat on my ass, and then we hoot so loud I'm surprised no one comes to check out the commotion.

We end up minutes later in a heap together on the floor, panting, Annie's head propped on my stomach, her heels on the sofa. I poke at her hair-sprayed bangs. They're fascinating. Like stiffened egg whites.

She jerks her head away and drops it back down, nailing me in the solar plexus. I grunt.

"Oh, shit. Did I hurt you?" She scrambles up to sitting, dopey-eyes wide with alarm.

"I'm fine."

"Did I hit the Franken-scar?"

"Nope. Lucky for you, fathead."

Annie snorts and settles back down.

I wish, for the one millionth time, that *it* wasn't there. The permanent backdrop to my life. The day I was gutted like a fish.

Doesn't matter where I am or what I'm doing, right behind me lurks the worst day of my life. Every memory I have, it's there, making every good time that came before it a calm before the storm, everything that came after a *could-have-never-been*.

And so many people have the picture of that day up in their heads, in living color. At least five people I see on a daily basis have seen the inside of my chest cavity. That's a fact of my life. I haven't even seen five real live dicks in my life, but there are at least a handful of people out there who know what my spleen looks like.

And me? I'm missing huge chunks. Not of those hours in the garage. I can't scrub that from my mind. But afterwards. There are days, weeks missing. And it's like this terrible thing happened, everyone knows about it, no one talks about it, and I've spent a decade trying to piece it back together or *come to terms with it*—whatever that means—or shove it out of my mind. But I can't. There's a permanent reminder skulking at the edges of my life, a threat I can never talk about, never escape.

I wish I could watch what happened like a movie. Force myself to see it all from every angle, force myself to relive every moment one last time until I can understand it, move on. Deal only with *now*, put *then* away on a shelf.

"Annie? What do you remember?" I startle her. She's on her phone, texting someone. Bullet, probably.

"What do you mean?"

"That day. When you came to the hospital. What do you remember?"

"Shit, Crista. You want to talk about that now?"

"I remember it happening. Then I passed out. I kind of remember Scrap and Dad finding me. The other guys showing up. That prospect was there. The one who moved to Florida?"

"Axel?"

"Yeah. Him. He threw up. I remember Scrap leaning on me hard to put pressure on the wound, and Dad crying. And then there's pretty much a blank for, like, weeks."

"It's a blessing."

"That's what people say."

"You don't think so?"

"I want to know what you remember."

"Again?" Annie kind of groans.

I go through these phases every so often. I want to confront the past. Get what closure I can. I get a little fixated for a while. Eventually, I give up, go back to guarding the life I have. Tell myself that's acceptance.

Annie knows the drill. She humors me now.

"You were totally out of it. You looked like a mummy. Your head was wrapped up, and everything else from the neck down. They had a nurse sitting next to your bed 'cause every time you woke up, you fought. Fucked up the IV and the wires and shit. Everything would start beeping. It freaked me the fuck out."

"Did I say anything?"

"Not at the beginning. Not when I was there. Later you asked for stuff. Water or graham crackers. Your phone."

"Did I talk about it? What happened?"

Annie shrugs. "Mom said don't bring it up. And before they found him—Inch—they were worried about the cops. Everybody was worried you'd say something, and Inch would end up in custody."

"How did they know it was Inch?" My heartbeat ratchets up a notch. I don't usually flirt this close with the truth.

Annie sighs. "You know. The club was out looking for you, and that homeless guy said he'd seen Inch driving around. Little while later Gus spots Inch hauling ass down Route 12. They lose him, so they backtrack. Find you."

"And I didn't say anything about who it was?"

"Nah. You were hella out of it. Good thing Gus saw Inch. If he didn't, we might never have found you. Never known who did it."

I've thought about that. What if no one ever knew who did it? Scrap would be free. Maybe married with kids. My stomach lurches; I think with guilt.

And if Inch was never caught? Would I have ever worked up the courage to hunt him down? Kill him? Shoot him? Do it up close, gut him like he gutted me?

No. I wouldn't have. At heart, I'm a coward. I've known for years now that I don't have what it takes to kill a man.

Inch is dead, though. Long dead. Scrap Allenbach killed him with his bare hands.

After I was left me for dead, they found me bleeding out on the floor of an abandoned gas station on Route 12. I was in the ICU for nine days. The doctors didn't think I'd make it. While I was in a medically-induced coma, the whole club beat the bushes for Inch Johnson.

My Dad, Scrap, and Nickel found him drinking a beer at the Pylestown Inn. Scrap beat Inch to death in front of a dozen witnesses while Nickel held my Dad back, pinned to a wall.

While I was unconscious in a bed, Scrap killed the man who put me there. What if I'd been awake? Could I have changed things? Or would I have let it slip, my secret, and sent another man—my dad, Heavy, Bullet—off to ruin his life, destroy his future, over my stupidity?

The *what ifs* are enough to drive you mad. Or hate yourself.

I change the subject. "Did he come to see me? In the hospital?"

"Who? Scrap?"

"Yeah."

Annie hums. "The whole club was there at first. In the waiting room. Then the doctor said you weren't gonna make it, and everyone went in to say goodbye. Mom lost her shit. Kicked everyone out. Then two or three days later, the doctor said you might pull through. At that point, everyone had kind of settled into shifts. Aunt Shirl was bein' a boss bitch."

I remember. Aunt Shirl still worked at Petty's Mill General then. She sat with me after her shifts, reading *Ladies Home Journal*. I remember finding that weird since Aunt Shirl's kind of a feminist, not really the Suzy Home-maker type.

"Was Scrap there?"

"All the guys were. Except Axel. That dude bolted."

"Did he seem really upset?"

"I'm guessing so if he left town, never to return."

"Not Axel. I mean Scrap."

"Everyone was upset."

I huff. Getting Annie to talk is like pulling teeth, but at

least she'll talk about it. No one else is remotely open to rehashing the past with me.

"Was he more upset than the other guys?"

Annie shrugs. "Obviously. Considering he went and killed the motherfucker."

"I mean at the hospital. Was he—like—obviously in a homicidal rage?"

It's Annie's turn to groan. "It was forever ago. I don't remember. What are you really asking, Crista? You asking why Scrap did it?"

I hold my breath. Yeah. Maybe I am.

"He was crazy in love with you, dumbass."

"He never said anything."

"He was twenty-one. You were sixteen."

"How do you know he was in love with me?"

Annie rolls her eyes. "How does anyone know? He was all up in your business. Giving you rides home from band practice."

"Dad made him do that. He was a prospect."

"Didn't see Dad letting Axel ride you anywhere."

She has a point, but that speaks more to who Dad trusts than anything else. "Scrap never said anything to me back then. Never called me. No texts. No standing outside my window with a boombox."

"He beat the shit out of Creech."

"Huh?"

"You don't remember that? Creech told some stupid, clarinet blow-job joke, and Scrap beat the shit out of him."

I remember that now. Vaguely. I thought the guys were just horsing around, sparring. The younger brothers do that a lot.

"That doesn't mean anything."

Annie wriggles, combing the carpet with her freaky toes. A real languid note has entered her voice. She's totally high.

"What's this all about, little sister?"

I exhale. "I didn't know what to say to him out there. I *don't* know what to say to him."

"Oh, baby. You don't have to say anything."

"Obviously, I do." I remember the disapproval on Heavy's face. Harper's scowl. The sweetbutt who said I should have at least welcomed him home.

"Tell him he looks hot as shit."

My face heats. He does. He's in a whole other league of hot. Like a guy from the calendar Ernestine has hanging in the kitchen.

"I'm too shy."

"Tell him anyway. The way he was looking at you—" She drifts off.

"The way he was looking at me what?"

"He wants to hear you say it."

"Bullshit."

Annie doesn't dignify that with a response, and we get quiet, settle in. She relights the jay, and this time when she passes it to me, I take a drag. I try to exhale in perfect rings, but it's been way too long.

"You are so lame." Annie mouths a perfect oval.

"I'm not the one texting Bullet Nowicki for a booty call."

"You would be if you knew what you were missing."

I raise my eyebrows. "A lifetime of disappointment?"

"And nine inches of perfect, albeit fleeting, satisfaction."

"Oh, gross!" I knock her shoulder with mine, and we're giggling again when there's a soft tap at the door.

"Yes! I bet that's my nine inches now. Come on in, baby."

"Is that who you were texting?"

I'm totally dope-slow, so Annie manages to half-crawl,

half-lunge to the door and open it before I can drag her
back. A wall of music and laughter rolls in, and I'm bracing
for a dose of the world's worst decision when I catch a
glimpse of gray T-shirt and a half smile.

He slips in so quick, a beer in his hand, that I don't have
time to do more than freeze, sitting on the floor in front of
the sofa with my knees tucked to my chest and a joint in
hand.

"Scrap! Join us!" Annie makes a welcome sweep with her
arm and scoots back to nestle next to me, relieving me of the
joint while she stretches and crosses her long legs.

With a soft chuckle, Scrap comes in, gently shutting the
door behind him, muffling everything but the thump of the
bass. He eyes the sofa behind us and Mom's desk chair, and
then after a second, he lowers himself, propping his back
against the wall. He drapes his forearms on top of his
drawn-up knees, dangling his beer from one strong hand.

He's so long, so much man, he shrinks the room. A
feeling close to panic, but pricklier, kind of bubbly even,
rises in my chest. I've never felt this before.

"Is this a private party?" Scrap smiles all lop-sided, and
the prickles go crazy.

"Yup. Invitation only." Annie's so stretched out, she can
nudge Scrap's boots with her bare feet, which she does.
"New boots?"

God, even Scrap's feet are huge, especially laced up in
brand new black shit-kickers. Of course, they're new. His
whole outfit must be. 'Cause prison. I dig my elbow into
Annie's side.

"Yup," he says.

Annie leans forward, offering the jay to Scrap. He shakes
his head, taking a sip from his beer instead.

"Harper buy 'em for you?" Annie's always real worried

about what Harper Ruth is up to. They were in the same class at school, and it's a weird relationship. Annie's always comparing herself to Harper, Harper always comes out better in the comparison, and Annie's perpetually left feeling second rate. They say they're friends, though. I don't get it.

Scrap shrugs. "I don't know. They were at Heavy's house." He answers Annie, but his eyes are on me. A warmth creeps up my chest. I squirm.

"You went there?" Annie asks. "After you got out?"

"Yeah. We had a few drinks. I got a shower."

"That must've felt great."

"Yeah. It was awesome."

What would that look like? Scrap in the shower. No shirt. Hot water. Eyes closed. Bent with his hand around his — Oh, shit. What is my mind doing? My brain doesn't go there. Not ever. Not even when I try to make it. My skin heats all over, and I start to sweat. I wrap my arms tighter around my knees.

My wonky brain throws up another picture. Scrap under a stream of water, head tilted back, beads streaming down the cords in his neck, and I miss a breath. I swallow hard, but my mouth is bone dry, so I cough, a real hack, and it keeps going on and on.

Scrap holds out his beer. I ignore it. I try to hold my breath, force my lungs to quit going crazy. And then he scoots closer, so close that he can press the cold beer against my hand, and he holds it there until I take it.

Fuck. He's so close now. He's not across the room— although the office is so small, it's not like across the room was far enough. He's near enough to touch me. I catch myself leaning toward him. What was that?

I hack again, and then sip the beer slowly. His lips were

here. Now mine are, and he's staring, so he knows. He might be thinking the same thing. That my lips are touching where his were. A wave of heat unfurls in my body, rolling from my chest down my arms and legs.

If I drink much more, I'll finish it, but it's so hard to hand it back. I feel better with something in my hand. Anxiety and self-consciousness and this weird awareness are messing with my head.

I'm not used to bodies. My own. Other people's. I try not to think about them. Notice them. Wonder about them.

This whole scenario should be fucking with a lot of my triggers. Scrap and I aren't alone, per se, but it's only Annie here, and he's really big and between me and the door. It's not total darkness, but it's dim, and we're far away from the crowd. I'm sitting, and I'm buzzed, not the prime position to be able to run if I had to.

The urge to check rises in me, but it's stupid, so I force it down. I'm good. Annie is right here. Dad and Mom are down the hall. And this is Scrap. He's freaking me out, but it's not in the usual way. My body's primed, but not to fight or run. I shift in my seat. I need to move, but where?

It's like Annie senses my disquiet, and she lays her head on my shoulder. "So how's the homecoming so far?" she asks.

"Good. Good." Scrap smiles politely, but his eyes hold something heavy. "A girl got salty with me, though."

I lower my eyes, bite the inside of my cheek. "I'm sorry."

"It was my fault. I said something dumb about her hair."

Again, I can't help it. I reach up and brush a lock behind my ears with nervous fingers. I'm grateful for the dim lighting. The mess I've become—the extra pounds, the obvious lack of effort—it's harder to make out with the shadows and my bulky clothes.

"You didn't really say anything bad." He didn't. I do look different. A lot different. It's part camouflage, part what happens when for a long time, your life was a cycle of surgery, recovery, and episodic depression.

"I didn't say what I meant."

The room's grown so quiet, the hollering and throbbing bass from outside is like a bubble around us, and inside, the air's still. Even Annie's relaxed, her breath slow and even, her head nods toward her chest. I think she's falling asleep.

"What did you mean?" I whisper, half because Annie's nodding off and half because this conversation feels somehow like a secret.

"That I missed you."

An ache blossoms in my chest. "How could you miss me? You hardly knew me."

He exhales. "Shit, Crista. I followed you around for, like, months."

He did? "We never talked."

"Pig Iron would've cut my balls off. You were underage."

I don't know what to do with this. Shivers are racing over my skin, and I don't even know what churning, bubbling thing is happening in my belly. A lot of times, my mind can't keep up with the ways my body goes haywire.

"Well, I hardly knew you." I don't want to be so mean, but I can't help it. I can't talk and handle what's happening inside me at the same time.

"I get that. Don't change nothin'. Still missed you."

"Don't you hate me?"

"No."

"Why not? I'm the reason you were in there."

"No, you wasn't. I made my own choices." He says it so plain. Like it's the simple truth.

"I didn't ask you to do it."

"I know."

"I wish you hadn't." My voice cracks. Annie snuggles closer, wedging her head in the crook of my neck. I wonder if she's faking?

"I ain't got no regrets." That's a lie. I *know* he does. He said so.

"What do you want from me?" I know I must sound spiteful. Ungrateful. I can't help it, though. We're only talking, but my body thinks it's an emergency.

Maybe it's my quasi-hysterical tone that finally forces Scrap's patience to slip. His face loses its stillness, comes alive. He drums the fingers of one hand on the side of his leg.

"Can't we just talk?"

"About what? Why?"

"Shit, Crista. I don't know." He exhales heavily. "Maybe I want to get to know you."

What?

"Get to know me? Like what? A date?" I can't believe I said that.

"Sure."

"You want to go out with me?"

"If you want. We can go somewhere nice."

He can't mean that. *Not as sorry as I am.* That's what he said at SCI Wayne. An unexpected wave of anger ambushes me, sweeps away the weird feelings, leaving me tense and brittle.

"I don't do that."

"Do what? Go on dates?" He sounds oddly pleased. "Why not?"

I raise my hand to indicate...all of it. "Well, for one, no one asks."

His jaw tightens. "And if they did?"

I shrug. "It's a non-issue."

"Why?"

Seriously?

"Why?" he pushes, and my face throbs, half embarrassment, half this bizarre fury. What is with this guy? He needs me to say it?

If it were anyone else, any other time, I'd bail. I'm not one who shares. I can't be. But tonight, I'm on edge from the weeks of waiting for today, from the hours that felt like years while we waited around for him to roll up tonight. His "why" tips me over, and I go off.

"Who wants to date the hard luck story?"

His face hardens. "Crista." He looks so disappointed. Fuck him.

"Crista, what? You're the one who came in here. You're the one who asked."

Annie's head is too light against my shoulder. She's definitely faking it, but she's not about to stop me from running off at the mouth. She's probably loving this.

"Crista..." He squints like he's trying to read my face, but it's dim in here. I yank my hood forward and jerk back so I'm as far from him as the sofa will allow.

"It's a small town. No one wants to go out with the poor girl from the evening news."

"Crista." The disappointment in his voice is turning into something even worse. Pity. Raw and ugly.

"It is what it is. Life sucks, man."

I screw up my courage and glare directly at him, hard, willing him to get up, leave, stop sitting there all strong and tough while I flail around in my stupid self-pity and useless rage like some spiteful troll.

This is *bullshit*. I don't feel this way. People pity me, but that's their M.O. Not mine. I get through the day. I know the value of each fucking one. And he strolls in here, and all of a sudden, my life's a sob story? *Fuck.*

He tilts his head back and rests it against the wall. He's silent a long moment before he sighs. God, I hope this is it. This is when he gives up and goes away.

"Shit, Crista. I shoulda never done it."

I thought I'd accepted it, his regret, but still, the fact of it knocks the breath from my lungs. He's right. He shouldn't have. I know this, but the guilt cuts so deep, my eyes sting.

"Yeah. It wasn't worth it." Can't this just be over?

"Huh?" He shakes his head. "No. I mean I should have never sent you away, told you I didn't want to see you. I was bein' a pussy. See, when you first go in, it's—Nevermind. That don't matter now. What matters is...I thought you'd be okay. I fucked up."

My brain offers up a fragment of memory. A plastic chair. The faint scent of bleach and metal. My broken sobs echoing against pale green tiles and his hard, blank face. *Not as sorry as I am.*

His face isn't blank now. Not anymore. There's anger there, almost crowding out the pity. "I trusted you were taken care of. I was wrong. I'm gonna fix that."

"What are you even talking about?"

"I'm gonna make this right." He tries to meet my gaze. Hold it tight. "I'm gonna get you straight."

The words feel like a backhand. I mean, I *know* I'm a loser, but at least Annie and Mom and Dad and everyone else in my life have the tact not to rub my face in it.

Still, it *stings*, so when I answer, I swing wild. "How? What are you gonna do for me?"

Annie grunts and wriggles herself back upright, trying to calm me down and rouse herself fully awake at the same time.

Scrap's calm is totally fled. His hands are fisted, his eyes flashing. He's pissed, barely holding it in, and part of me is ugly and glad. He's gonna pity me? No. I feel sorry for *him*.

"You can keep your savior bullshit, you know? I'm fine. You take care of yourself."

I struggle to stand, careful to stay as far from him as I can, and then I duck past him and haul ass as soon as I'm up.

He's getting to his feet, stepping forward while I bolt, and even though I'm racing away, plowing through drunk brothers and dancing sweetbutts, the fear still nails me like a wrecking ball. The outline of a man, looming. A malevolent presence at my back. *Gasoline and piss. Cold concrete. Copper.*

I can't hear what he says, but I can see him shake his head.

Like *how sad*.

Like *crazy bitch*.

I can't believe I blew up balloons for this shit. My own goddamn pity party.

5

SCRAP

About four in the morning, I lay Nickel out with an uppercut. I been takin' all comers by the sand pit since Crista ran off, so the odds were 3:1 against me. Guess my brothers figured I'd be tired out by now. Guess they figured wrong.

Don't know where these rednecks are gettin' these fat rolls, but I ain't gonna complain. It's nice having cash on hand that doesn't feel like a hand out.

I offer Nickel a hand, but he groans and waves me off. At least one thing's the same. That fucker's still insane. It was a good fight. No pulled punches. I wander back toward the clubhouse, my gait none too steady. I been workin' on a bottle of Jack in between rounds.

At least the sweetbutts stayed back at the pit. Shakin' 'em off has been tweakin' my nerves. I turn one down, two show up to take her place. They ain't what I want.

Shit. This whole scene is gettin' to me. It's so damn *loud*.

The party's still goin' hard, but all I want is peace and quiet. I want to pass out on a bed somewhere without a dude jerkin' off in a bunk beneath me and fluorescent lights flickering overhead, but I ain't nowhere close to bein' able to sleep. I figured takin' a few beatings would wear me out, but it only fed the sick feeling that's bloomed in my guts ever since I caught sight of Crista behind that bar.

I didn't even realize it was her at first. No one said she'd picked up weight and gone butch or whatever the fuck you call it. Short hair. Men's clothes. That was a surprise, but whatever, I get it. After what happened, she don't want to draw no attention to herself.

Her looks ain't the only thing that's changed, though. Not by far. She's worn out now. Faded. In that room, I would've never picked her out if Charge hadn't pointed to her. She's like the dudes inside who you don't notice when they come and go. Months later, you're like, "When did Joe get out?" And everyone's like, "Who?"

God, Crista Holt used to be a fuckin' *picture*. I warned off so many pissants, sniffin' around, checkin' her out. She had these tiny freckles across her cheeks. Always wore pink lip gloss and blue eyeshadow which made her look even younger than she was. I felt like such a dirty fuck 'cause I never could stop watchin' her. She was real shy, but Annie'd make her giggle till she couldn't stop, and when Deb and the other old ladies bossed her, she'd swish her walk with just the smallest touch of sass.

The sick in my belly turns full sour, and I stumble through the back door into the clubhouse. A chorus of "Scrap!" greets me, and a drunken arm is slung around my shoulder.

Grinder huffs over, starts shoutin' some story at me, drunk as shit, and a couple sweetbutts I don't recognize saunter over. Damn. I just want a place to rest my carcass. Regroup. Figure out what the hell even happened back in Deb's office.

And then an enormous paw claps me on the shoulder, and everyone steps back. It's got to be Heavy. Dude's the only one I know who's got a wake when he moves.

"My office?" Heavy raises an unopened bottle of Johnnie Walker.

I nod and follow him to the annex, down the corridor Crista raced through a few hours back like her ass was on fire. This part of the clubhouse is all new since I went away. It used to be a fenced in yard for shit meant for the dump.

I hear bootsteps behind us, so I ain't surprised when Charge and Forty follow us in to Heavy's office, takin' seats around a huge, wood coffee table, each guy gravitating to a certain chair like dudes inside at mealtime.

Damn, I been gone a long time. I ain't got an assigned seat.

There's an engine sittin' on a drop cloth on a side table. There's enough room next to it, so I prop my ass up there.

Heavy snorts. "Guess I need to get more chairs."

"He can sit on Forty's lap." Charge kicks his feet up onto the coffee table. Forty flips him the bird, and it cracks me up. Forty got out of the service on a medical discharge a few years back, but they ain't been able to take the Army out of the man. Watchin' him give the finger is like seein' one of those guards at Buckingham Palace scratch his jock.

"Maybe next time." I wink at Forty. No reaction. Dude is a stone.

Heavy throws me the Johnnie Walker, and I catch it. Check the label. "Blue? When I went away, we was happy with Red."

"Times have changed." Heavy lights a stogie, shakes the match.

"I can see that." Heavy's dad was still president when I

went upstate, and Slip Ruth didn't have no fancy office. He ran shit from the pool table beside the bar.

"Expense ain't much of a concern no more." Forty pulls his own cigar from his breast pocket, offers it to me. I decline. Never was one for smokin'.

"'Our barns are filled with plenty, and our vats are bursting with wine.'" Heavy leans back and folds his hands over his gut like some fat pasha.

"What's that? Book of Genesis?" I guess.

"Proverbs."

Heavy's been quotin' the Bible since we was in school. His ma, Miss Linda, was a real Christian woman before she hooked up with Slip Ruth, and she had a verse for every occasion.

"You got a job for me, then?"

The club's been keepin' my commissary topped off this whole time, and I know they'll float me as long as I need, but seein' Crista, I'm gettin' anxious. I'm gonna need a way to take care of her, 'cause I'll be damned if shit's gonna keep goin' like it seems to have been.

"No rush, man. Settle in. Relax." Heavy waves his hand like it's nothin'.

I force my voice to stay even. "Sounds real good, brother, but I need a way to pay my bills."

I don't know what I said, but Charge and Forty both bark a laugh.

"You're covered, man," Forty says.

"I ain't no fuckin' charity case."

"Simmer down, brother." Heavy taps the ash of his cigar. "Your dividends are in the bank."

"Huh?"

"From the company. We told you this. All patched-in members get a cut from Steel Bones LLC now. You've got a nice nest egg. I invested for you. Went big in ride sharing and porn sites." Heavy winks.

"Pig Iron said there was some set aside for me. I figured it would be a few hundred."

"We ain't makin' runs for peanuts no more." Charge gestures around the place. It is hella nicer than when I went away. Wide screen hangin' on the wall. Recessed lighting.

"Crista know I got money in the bank?" I ask.

The brothers share a look.

"It's club business. We don't publish it, but it's common knowledge." Forty lifts a shoulder. "We've had to get kind of particular about the club pussy. Lots of gold diggers sniffin' around. Lookin' for an eighteen-year free ride."

"Why do you ask?" Heavy leans forward. He ain't dense. He can feel the turn in the conversation.

"Something she said earlier. She was pissed at the time, though."

"What she got to be pissed about?" Forty's tone ain't unfriendly, but it still raises my hackles.

"Ain't your concern."

Forty raises his hands. "No offense meant, my brother."

I ease up. Take a breath. These are my brothers. Whatever they've let happen, it ain't been out of malice.

"With Crista...this all has thrown her off." Heavy's bein' careful with his words. He needs to be. The shit between Crista and I is just that. Between us. I wish there was more we had—some piece left from before—but if that meltdown in Deb's office is it for now, well, it's where I begin.

"She got every right to be thrown," I say, and to a man, they shift uneasy in their chairs. They know they've dropped the ball. "Wish I'd had a heads up, though. Ain't like I didn't ask. Every visit. You said she was good. This what y'all call good?"

There's a quiet that descends on the room so thick you could lift it.

"Well?"

"In comparison...yes." Heavy's searchin' for the right way to say it, but my patience is past run out.

"You said she was doing *great*. Got her own place. Workin'. Takin' classes. Got a dog. You made it sound like she was a fuckin' co-ed, spring break at the beach, the whole nine."

"We ain't lied to you, brother," Charge says.

"Where she livin'?" In my head, she's got one of those apartments over in Shady Gap that they rent to singles who work in Pyle. A place with a pool and a gym. Maybe with a roommate she goes out with to karaoke like the people on sitcoms.

Heavy answers me this time. "Pig Iron put in one of those mother-in-law apartments over his garage."

Not what I'd imagined. "What classes did she take? Where at?"

"I don't know. Them G.E.D. classes. Online. To get her diploma."

"She didn't fuckin' graduate?"

Heavy's slow-shaking his wooly head. Despite the interest in boxing, I'm at core an even-tempered man, but damn if my blood ain't startin' to pound in my ears. They promised me she was good.

"You don't understand," he says. "There were a lot of surgeries at first. They had to put her back together, and then there were all these follow-ups."

"It was a long road, and she came through like a champ, but there was lot of time she was recovering from this or that," Charge takes over tryin' to explain, and he's the easy, charmin' one, but his *it's alright, it's all fine* schtick ain't makin' this sound better. It's makin' it sound like my brothers were keepin' shit from me.

"What do you mean, follow-ups?"

Forty steps in. You can hear it in his voice. He ain't got patience for sugar-coating shit neither. "She needed surgery twice for, uh, uh—"

"Obstructions. Of the large intestine," Heavy supplies.

"And they had to—" Forty circles his hand in front of his gut.

"She had a uterine reconstruction." Of course, Heavy knows the medical terms.

"What the f—No. Stop." I hold up a hand. No one told me shit about this. They said she was doin' well. At first, it was *she's feelin' better all the time.* Then she was *gettin' out more.* Then, she was *good. Real good.*

And damn, but I didn't ask too many questions, did I? Never asked to see a picture. Waved it off when a brother offered. It was too much, being stuck there, so far away with so much time to go. I thought if I saw her, I wouldn't be able to do the hours. The days.

To do real time, you got to narrow everything down to the box you're in. You think about time passing outside, you'll go crazy. I had to come out whole—for her, for Crista —so I got real good at living in the moment. The reps and sets, the pages and chapters, the playing cards or the tools I held in my hand.

When I thought about her, after lights out, I remembered pink lip gloss. Chipped purple nail polish on delicate hands, clutching a clarinet case. A sweet blush rising up her neck onto her freckled cheeks.

It was so hard to keep my face blank when I saw her earlier behind the bar. Dark circles under her eyes. Face pasty white. Chapped lips. The skin around her fingernails all red and chewed to shit. How that lime juice didn't burn her fingers like hell, I don't know.

This is a girl ain't no one takin' care of right.

I let my shoulders fall against the wall, and I take a deep, deep swig of whiskey. This is not how this day was supposed to go down. It's all wrong, and it's been wrong for so damn long.

I look at Heavy. "I need a job."

"Yeah, brother. Of course. I talked to Big George. He's gonna set you up at the Autowerks."

I did some automotive work on the inside, besides the restoration shit I used to do with my old man, but the thought of spending my days inside depresses the fuck out of me.

"I'd rather work on a crew. Roofing. Framing. Whatever."

Heavy glances quick at Forty then shifts in his seat. What was that?

"If it's all the same, I'd rather work outside," I say. "You get that."

"I do." Heavy nods. "It's just...anyone told you what's been going on with the Raiders?"

Nobody gossips as much as an MC. While we were waiting at my parole hearing, Pig Iron reenacted the whole scene at the Patonquin site when Knocker Johnson blew the place up with repurposed fireworks. He even did voices. Cue himself told me about how the Raiders sent two fuckers to trash The White Van, a tear in his eye for his shattered glassware.

"I heard some."

"Basically, Knocker's stirring shit up, lookin' for a little revenge."

"Eighteen years inside is a long time to only want a *little* revenge." I should know. If the fucker who put me there wasn't dead, my plans would be quite a bit different than get with my woman and start workin' construction.

Charge gives me a chin jerk. "That's what I've been sayin'. These two fuckers don't listen to me, though."

"Knocker's lettin' off some steam. It's only money. We wait him out. He'll find something better to do with himself." Heavy's sayin' the words, but even I can tell he don't believe 'em. What the fuck? Since when did we bullshit each other?

"He comes at me, I'm takin' him out." Just layin' that out there.

By all accounts, he had no knowledge of what Inch was up to when he attacked Crista. When that shit went down, Knocker had been inside several years already on charges from the blown job. The Rebel Raiders was Inches' club, his big "fuck you" to Steel Bones for what happened to his dad and brother when federal agents pulled over a truck and it turned out they were hauling guns under the crates of cigarettes they'd agree to run across state lines.

Far as I know, Knocker never patched in to the Raiders. He served his time at Wayne, same as me, but he was up the hill at maximum. I heard shit through the grapevine. His dad passed. He blacked out his Steel Bones ink. I thought he was unaffiliated, but If he's looking to start where Inch stopped, I have no compunction about ending him.

"He ain't comin' at you. Listen." Heavy gets serious, leans forward in his chair, makin' it creak in protest. "The work we're doin' now, it ain't what Slip had us doin'."

Yeah. Slip mostly had us humpin' cigarettes into New York and providing protection for the Russians when they ran guns out to Chicago. Lots of time on the road. Not much construction.

"What are you sayin'?"

"I'm saying when you check out your bank account, you'll see we're not doing bitch work anymore. And we ain't makin' union construction wages, neither."

I don't follow. A few years after I went inside, brothers were always goin' on about how we were goin' legit. I didn't think too much about it. Didn't apply to my day-to-day.

"Steel Bones specializes in a very particular clientele with unique needs that require the utmost confidentiality." Heavy sounds like a fuckin' brochure.

"You mean Des Wade." He's the fat cat Harper's got her claws in, the kind of criminal who gets his picture taken with the mayor.

"He's a client. One of many."

"Make it clear for me. What are you sayin', Heavy?"

"I'm saying we run a different kind of organization now. Construction is the core business, and we fulfill a niche in the market. Our clientele pays a premium for discretion. Exits that don't appear on the papers filed with the county. Safe rooms and bunkers no one ain't never gonna talk about."

I don't think I can take the commercial much longer. "The point, Heavy?"

He sighs. "I can't have a parole officer showin' up on a job site."

Fuck.

This goddamn day.

"Big George is so fuckin' stoked to have you up at the Autowerks," Charge chimes in. "He misses your dad."

Yeah. So do I. Shit, I miss Big George, too. He was the one who gave me my road name. My dad was a welder, and when I was born, Big George took to calling me Scrap as a joke. The name stuck.

"Still, I'd rather be outside."

"Hey, you want fresh air and sunshine? Have a prospect push the car out in the front lot. Work out there." Forty's face is dead serious.

"That's some fuckin' redneck shit, Forty."

"Well, I am a fuckin' redneck, ain't I?" He raises his flask to me, and after a moment, I lift my near empty bottle. Charge and Heavy join in, and the mood eases up.

"We got you all set upstairs." Charge changes the subject. "My old lady Kayla decked it out real nice. New mattress. Flat screen. It's got an en suite."

"What the fuck's 'en suite?'" Forty asks.

"Shitter attached to the bedroom." Everyone looks at me. "What? We had HGTV at Wayne."

"You get all the channels?"

"Hell, yeah. HBO. HEPC. All of 'em."

The conversation goes right stupid from there, and much later, the sun comes up, turnin' the room mellow gold, swirling clouds of cigar smoke thick in the air. There's a burn in the back of my throat from the whiskey, and the laughing, and even though my ribs ache and my knuckles are busted to hell—even though Crista Holt don't want me and ran from me scared—there's a lightening in my soul.

I'm home with my brothers. Things changed, but not that.

About seven or eight, when everyone's stumbled off to find themselves a place to crash or some willing pussy, I sober up and decide to take a ride down the Emmorton Road. It's a great riding road, long stretches where you can open up that lead into wicked twists, winding through tall corn fields and gnarled woods, hardly any signs of life except the farmhouses set off way back.

It's been ten years, but the road's the same, smooth despite the patched-up asphalt, no yellow lines, no shoulder. Last time I rode this way, I was a young man. I ain't that old now, but I feel ancient. Petrified like wood turned to stone.

I was a kid when I went inside. I thought like a kid. It took getting jumped by five Aryan Brotherhood assholes, five dudes bigger and meaner and more fucked in the head than anyone I'd known before, to make me a man. To teach me the truth in what my dad had told me a few months before he passed.

In the middle of a shady wood, where the road takes nearly a ninety-degree angle, I pull off at the old Calvary Baptist church. The building's been shuttered since I was a kid. My mom used to drag me here with Grandma Allenbach on Christmas and Easter. I hated it. No heat in the winter, and too many strange ladies fussing over me. The church built a new place over in Shady Gap shortly after Grandma passed, and they've let this place go to rack and ruin.

I back in to the parking lot, lower the kick stand, and make my way behind the church to the small graveyard. Someone's been mowing here, but they ain't put in too much effort. High grass grows at the edges of the clearing, and brown leaves lie thick on the ground.

The Allenbachs are at the far end. Grandma and Pops have proper stones, but all we could afford when Ma passed was a marker. When Dad went so sudden, the club bought a nice headstone with room for both their names, but no one ever thought to take Mom's marker away. It's flat between the two larger stones, edged in clumps of grass the weedwhacker missed. I crouch and start with that.

This could be a sad place, a sad moment, but it ain't. It's peaceful out here. It smells musty, like living things.

I trace Ma's dates with a finger. She was twenty-six when she died. Five years younger than I am now.

It was cervical cancer, caught much too late. Comin' up, we didn't have money for doctors unless you were on death's door. By the time Ma felt bad enough to spend the money, the cancer had worked its way to her lungs and bones.

At the end, she spent all her time in bed, propped up, mostly unconscious. I'd get home from school, grab my comforter and a snack, and make myself a place at the end of the bed, turning the TV to cartoons.

When Dad got home from the garage, he'd stomp into the bedroom, kiss whatever old lady had been watchin' Ma on the lips and send her home, and then, covered in grease and dirt, he'd climb into bed, boots still on. He'd bark at me to "Turn that shit to wrestling and get me a beer."

Ma would rouse a little, nestle into his side, and bitch at him for getting her sheets filthy. He'd pat her shoulder, kiss her forehead, and say, "Go back to sleep, baby. It's all handled."

A few days before she died, she wanted him to take her to the back porch. We lived in a shitty little rancher down on the flats, but the view from the back wasn't bad. There was a patch of woods and soybean fields.

Dad carried her out, and sat out there for hours, cradling her on his lap, whispering some shit to her that I couldn't overhear while he chain-smoked, holding his cigarette to her lips every once in a while.

After she passed, and we buried her here, he'd ride us out every so often. He'd always say, "Fuck. Should've stopped for flowers." But we never did. We'd stand here for a time, silent, as if we were waiting for something. Once, not too long before he had the heart attack, he broke the silence.

"How old are you now?"

"Thirteen."

"Old enough, I guess."

I didn't know for what, and I didn't ask.

"You know, boy, people act like a man is a man 'cause of what he can do."

"Yeah?"

"That ain't it, though. A man is a man 'cause of what he can bear."

I didn't say anything. What would I have said?

"A man can bear anything if he don't give in under the weight."

It wasn't until I got locked up that I understood what he meant. When my face was slammed into the concrete of the yard, and I saw ten years looming in front of me, day after day of pacing a cage between sudden, brutal fights for my life, that I understood what I needed to do to survive. I couldn't give in to the weight of it all. I had to bear it. And I could do that 'cause of Crista Holt.

Crista don't understand this, but I been living for her for ten years already. Shit, longer than that even. I've borne what can hardly be borne, for her. I ain't walkin' away 'cause shit ain't easy.

If I don't love Crista Holt, I don't know what I am. It's that simple.

And I guess, since she can hardly stand the sight of me, it's that fuckin' sad, too.

6

CRISTA

I back into a spot at the far end of the parking lot of Finnegan's Ice Cream. It's early in the day, too early for Finnegan's to be open. I'm the only car in the lot. I leave the engine on, but I put it in neutral and yank up the emergency break.

My heart quickens, and a cold sweat breaks out all over my skin. I tug the zipper of my hoodie to the very top, pull it forward so my face is totally hidden.

The empty lot is spooky, but this early in the morning is a good time to watch the gas station across the street. It's morning rush hour, so there's lots of activity on Gracy Avenue. I watch the action in my rearview. They're busy like always.

Not many places that have full service anymore, but this place does. Lots of Buicks and Lincolns pull up real slow, older drivers taking the time to chat up the guy working the pumps, causing cars waiting for the self-service lanes to back up onto the road.

There's a lot of honking. Each time, my stomach leaps

into my throat. I'm jittery, but okay. I'm handling it. Every minute or so I pop the glove box and check the Beretta.

After this, I'm gonna drive out to the Autowerks. Deb needs me to pick up payroll for her. It's been a week since Scrap's party, and everything's more or less gone back to normal. He's tried to talk to me a few times while I've been workin' the bar. I try to think of something normal to say, fail, and end up giving him a beer and that's all. Last night, he didn't bother and bailed as soon as he saw me. Spent his evening sparring out by the fire pit.

Everyone's started shooting me half-dirty, half-pitying looks. Boots got drunk and asked me why I'm busting Scrap's balls. I'm not. I'm embarrassed and tongue-tied, and I have no desire to make it worse, which is the only thing opening my mouth can do. Besides, it's no one else's business, even though everyone's making it theirs. Ernestine tried to get me to take Scrap a plate of brownies from her the other day. When I asked if her legs were broken, she swatted me upside the head, and Grinder said, "See what I have to deal with? She's fuckin' violent."

Now Grinder's gonna be stinking up my place for at least another month, minimum.

The man pumping gas lunges for a squeegee, and from pure instinct, I startle, dragged out of my head by a jolt of adrenaline. The seat belt engages and digs into my neck, hard. Damn. My nerves are shot. Not like they're usually solid, but this is bad, even for me.

I ride the panic, let it ebb away, and watch the guy wash the windshield of an F150. Cars come and go. People duck into the convenience store, come out with coffee. A mechanic shows up and tugs open the bay doors. I gulp and acid scores my throat. I should have popped a Tums before I came.

I make myself keep looking. You can see inside the garage. Two cars up on lifts. The concrete floor. The work-benches.

The man at the pump waves up the next car, leans his scabbed elbows on the open driver's side window to chat.

My body fights me—heart sputtering, legs jiggling so hard my knees hit the steering wheel—but I make myself stay put. Five minutes is counting down on my phone.

Last time I came to watch a man pump gas was when Dad told me Scrap might be getting out. I didn't have to force myself to stay that day; I had to make myself leave.

I wonder a lot about what Dr. Ang would say if she knew I did this. She's big on exposure therapy. She's always talking about how I could go to the bookstore in Pyle. Baby steps. Start by getting in the car. Don't force it. Keep trying. Go a little further each time.

It's weirdly soothing to listen to her describe how you can very slowly work yourself up to go to a bookstore. I'm never gonna do it—I know it, she's got to know it on some level—but hearing about it is really calming.

Dr. Ang thinks my anxieties have become full-blown phobias because I'm not "doing the work." She also says I have PTSD. Depression. Body dysmorphic disorder. She's probably right. That's not why I am the way I am, though, why I stick to the places and people I know. I do that 'cause I'm not stupid.

Stupid is people walking through life believing nothing truly bad will ever happen to them. I mean, everyone knows about death. No one's surprised by the unavoidable bad shit, but I'm not talking about that. I'm talking about getting thrown into the back of a car when you're walking home from school one day, and then knowing, from that moment on, the exact joints where your body can tear easy, and where your bones will hold you together when your muscles are sliced apart.

That can happen.

So I'm not stupid. I know every entrance and exit in every place I go. I know which windows can be unlocked and how. Which I can fit through. Which I can reach, and if I can't, where there's a piece of furniture I can move for a leg up.

I know where the guns are kept. Where the gun safes are, what the combinations are. I know which drawer the wrenches are in and where the tire iron's hanging. I know which closet has the baseball bat, which side of the bed it's tucked under. I know where the phones are. I know where I can hide. I know all the ways to and from the businesses and the clubhouse, when stores along the way are open, the side streets, the alternate routes. I know this garage like the back of my hand.

I know that most of the time, I'm relatively safe, and I also know that can end at any time. The people I love are relatively safe, but all it'd take for that to end is for me to slip, blurt out the secret I keep like moldy Tupperware shoved in the back of the fridge, the ugliness I can't bear to think about, and I can never, ever confront.

So instead, I check my perimeter. Guarding this life that everyone thinks is so fucking small, and Scrap Allenbach might think is pathetic, but that I know is fragile as hell, balanced on the point of a needle.

My phone beeps, and I jerk against the seat belt again. Damn. I swipe the alarm off. My body's jacked up, but it's a familiar feeling. I figure I'll relax by the time I get to the Autowerks. I switch on the radio and search for something loud and angry. I find Megadeth, and I blare it until I pull into Big George's and park by the offices.

They've got all four bays open and working, and there's a good number of vehicles waiting for service. Wash is bending over an engine, and through the glass pane of the office, I can see Big George shooting the shit with Grinder and a man in a suit.

"Business is good. It's all good," I tell the knot in my stomach. Ease up. Cut me a break. Everything's fine.

Big George waves when he sees me, but he stops me halfway through the door.

"Crista! Deb said you'd be over. I got the payroll almost ready. Give me five. Do me a solid, though?"

"Sure thing."

"Can you run out to the hanger and get me the keys with the Lexus fob?"

I guess Big George and Grinder's legs are both broke again. "Sure thing, boss." I wave and head out back.

The hangar is a huge outbuilding set off behind the garage, well away from the main road. The bay opens in the back, facing the woods, but there's rooftop ventilation so the bay doors don't even have to be kept open. The hangar's where the boys work on the custom mods.

Some are projects for rich guys who don't want anyone to see their shit before it's finished. Some projects are cool little extras—Batmobile-type shit—for truly shady individuals from way out-of-town—as in Bogota or Moscow. That's how Steel Bones put their one percenter days behind them. Quality workmanship and the kind of discretion you get from brothers who'd die for each other without question. There's big money in the ability to keep your mouth shut.

I probably shouldn't know as much about it as I do, but like I said, Mom's the real bookkeeper, and since she's always got me doing her grunt work when the bar's slow, I hear a lot of shit.

I duck into the hangar through a side door and head for the wall where they hang the keys. There's not a lot going on today. Wall's trying to show Bucky something under the hood of a Hummer H1—they wave when I come in—and the only other vehicle is a sweet Indian Big Chief, the kind Steve McQueen rode. It's hot in the hangar. The bay door is down and the fans are off.

Which explains why Scrap Allenbach's not wearing a shirt when he comes out from the storage room with a bottle of water.

My whole body freezes and a wave of a heat crashes through me at the same time.

Oh, there's his shirt. Hanging from the back pocket of his jeans. At least these pants don't look straight from the store shelf like the ones he has been wearing. There's some grease on the thigh.

Scrap's got really solid thighs.

What the fuck am I doing? I'm checking him out. Shit. Did he notice?

He did. He's frozen in place, too, staring back, a drippy water bottle hanging from his hand. We're a good ten feet apart, but it feels like no distance at all.

His hair's mussy, as mussed as hair as short as his can get. He's sweaty, too.

"Hey." He seems to shake off the spell, and twists the cap of the water bottle. He chugs. His Adam's apple bobs. He looks like a commercial for Gatorade or a gym or something. I can't stop staring.

My hoodie suddenly feels really thick and scratchy.

"I'm just—" I point at the key rack. "Big George wants the Lexus keys."

Scrap's brow furrows. He closes the distance between us.

"The Lexus ain't in the hangar. The keys are up in the main office."

Oh. That jerk. It's another set up.

I see Scrap realize it at the same time. His mouth curls into that chagrined half-smile, and he glances down. "I'll remind George to mind his own business."

I shrug. I bet Mom had a hand in this, too. She was asking me the other day how Scrap was settling in. As if she thought I should know.

"Well...I guess I'll—" I point behind me to the door.

"Yeah." Scrap's smile is gone. That tight, give-nothing-away expression he's been wearing returns.

I should leave. There's nothing stopping me.

But maybe it's the residue from this morning at the gas station. Maybe I'm feeling crazy brave 'cause I lasted the whole five minutes without pissing myself.

Maybe it's the morbid curiosity that's been riding me lately, the kind that makes you stare when you drive past a wreck on the highway, even though you know you're an asshole for gawking, and all you're doing is hassling everyone else and making shit worse.

Maybe I just want to be here a little longer, feeling these weird squishy feelings float around in my belly.

"Can I ask you a question?"

Well, that fixed Scrap's face. His neutral expression is gone, replaced by a wariness. His eyes go bluer, and he flexes his jaw, nervous-like.

"Anything." He says it so serious.

A shiver zaps down my sweaty back. He means that. *Anything.* All of a sudden, whatever I was going to say flies out of my mind, and words just tumble out of my mouth.

"When you found me? With Dad and the others?"

"Yeah." His chest is rising and falling slow, as if he's breathing deep on purpose, while he waits for me to go on.

Oh, shit. I'm going to ask about that? I guess I am.

"Did I say anything?"

For a long moment, he stands there like a runner at the starting line, that same kind of full-body tension. Eventually, he seems to come to a decision.

"Will you sit?" His gaze darts around. There are two metal folding chairs by a workbench. He nods at them. They're close to the side exit. Wall and Bucky are still by the Hummer, maybe twenty-five feet away. The back door isn't too far.

Besides this is Scrap. He's safe.

Not for my mental well-being. Not at all. But he's not going to hurt me. This notched-up fear is my body being stupid. That's all.

I pat my phone in my pocket. My ankle sheath digs into my calf like always.

It's fine. Everything's fine. This is fine. I am fine.

I force myself to sit in a chair.

Scrap lowers himself next to me, and he's so long, he crowds me more than I expected. Even though his knee doesn't quite touch mine, I can feel him. Like a magnet. My skin hums with awareness, and I want to squirm, but if I do, I might bump him. I need to chill out. Breathe.

We're at an angle to each other, so I focus on the guys working instead of him staring at my face, and that eases my nervousness a bit. Not much, but some.

After a really long moment, he says, "I don't think you want to know."

"Yeah?" A pang of disappointment bursts in my chest. He's not going to tell me.

"*I* wouldn't want to know."

"I'm not you."

"Yeah. I been realizin' that."

"What's that supposed to mean?"

"I mean you're stronger than me, aren't you? All those years, I couldn't stand to see you, to look at what I was missin'. Hurt too bad. I was a pussy. You ain't scared of facin' shit though, are you?"

A face flashes in my mind. That's not true. I am afraid. All the time. I want to say so, but my brain's too full of what he said to form words. My heart is beating triple time, and I'm too gobsmacked by the idea that he thinks *I'm* stronger than *him*.

"You sure you want to know?"

He pauses again, giving me time to change my mind. I should change my mind. There's no good that comes from reliving the past, especially so close to a visit to Finnegan's Ice Cream, only the very real possibility of having a truly epic panic attack and giving Scrap a front seat to my crazy—but I nod instead.

"You asked for Deb."

What?

"You were crying *Mommy*. Over and over."

My chest aches like a mule kicked it. My nose tingles. My eyes burn. Those weird floaty feelings are gone.

I take it back. I don't want to know.

Scrap swallows. "Pig Iron kept telling you she'd be right there."

That was a lie. Mom was in Pyle that day on a girl's trip with Ernestine and Linda. I fold my arms around my middle, grab tight, try to hold on. He moves as if to touch me, and I flinch.

He stops. Takes a long sip of water. "Can I ask you a question now?"

What does he want to know? My uneasiness at the idea distracts me from my freak out, from the sadness that bloomed in my chest like a gunshot.

I glance up, meet his eyes. It's only fair.

"Do you remember that cookout?"

"Yeah." It was a few weeks before what happened, a birthday thing for Hobs. A family event.

Scrap and I played cornhole, and later, when most everyone was inside having cake, he pulled me into his lap when I walked past him toward the clubhouse. He brushed a kiss across my lips. I didn't know what to do, but I knew I wanted to be right where I was, so I stayed, blushing while he stroked my arm, until Annie yelled at me across the yard that Mom was coming outside.

That was a long time ago.

"Do you remember what you said?"

I shake my head.

"You were sittin' on my lap. Remember what you said?"

Of course not. I was sixteen, and I'd been sneaking sips from Annie's beers all day.

"First you said 'we shouldn't be doin' this. Dad'll cut your balls off.' Then you laid your cheek on my chest. You said I made a great chair except the part pokin' you in the ass." Scrap chuckles, real low. My cheeks flame.

"I did not say that."

"You did."

"I'd never say *balls*. Not back then."

"You were tipsy as hell. Cute, too."

He leans back in his chair. My eyes can't help but dart to his bare chest. The sweat has dried some, but his muscles are still slick and defined. My fingers twitch. I pull them into the cuffs of my hoodie.

"Why are you bringing this up?"

He skewers me with those blue eyes. "'Cause every time I remember that day at the garage, the only thing that keeps me sane is thinkin' about that other day, you in my arms, bitchin' about my hard-on."

It hurts. The words hurt. Missing the girl I was *hurts*.

"I can't remember what happened after the attack." I look at him, and I want him to tell me, but his blue eyes have gone unreadable again. "It drives me crazy. It's like, if I could only stitch all the pieces together, it'd make sense. But it's not going to, is it?"

Why does my voice sound so raw? Why am I even saying this shit?

He shifts. Cracks his neck. "On the inside, at Wayne? I wouldn't let myself remember. Only sometimes, and only the good shit. I saved up the good memories. Like for special occasions."

"How could you even stop yourself from thinking about it?" God, if only I could.

"Worked out a lot. Read the rest of the time."

"You read?" I don't know why this surprises me. Scrap's no brainiac like Heavy, but he's not a total dumbass like Creech or Bullet.

He nods.

"What?" I ask.

"What did I read?"

"Yeah."

He lifts a shoulder. "Whatever was on the cart. *All the President's Men*. Read that many times. Bob Vila's *Guide to Historic Homes of the South*. A lot of books by this chick Beatrice Small."

Hah. I can't imagine Scrap Allenbach reading historical romance. The idea must make me smile 'cause Scrap's focus drops to my lips, and he kind of leans forward. I draw my heels up to the edge of the chair and squish my tits to my chest with my knees.

"I read." I do. Way too much.

"Yeah? Bob Vila?"

I feel my lips twitch up again. "No. Action. Assassins. Spies."

"Like 007?"

"More La Femme Nikita."

"See. We have something in common."

"We're both literate?" I wince. Why can't I stop being a bitch to him?

"Hey, it's a start."

"To what?" The bitterness is back, so strong I can taste it in the back of my mouth. He doesn't answer me, gazes off instead so when he speaks again, he's not looking at me anymore.

"I know you're pissed at me." His voice is calm. Gentle, even. I squirm. I'm hot, and this chair is hard and uncomfortable.

"Why would I be pissed at you?"

"I left you. I sent you away."

I suck in a breath so hard I almost choke. The truth slams me, along with a bolt of rage. He *did*. He left me, told me to fuck off when I was sobbing in a stupid plastic chair and everything still hurt so fucking bad. I know he didn't have to be there for me when he was so down himself, but couldn't he have?

And I *know* it's not fair and I'm an ungrateful cunt, but still.... It's like he's cracked my heart open and peeled the lid back and now it's all open to the air, and it reeks and it's rotten, and I can hardly stand myself.

"You didn't owe me anything," I manage.

"Not true. You were mine to take care of, and I never

did."

"I wasn't yours."

"You can say that." Scrap sucks his cheek. "Don't make it true."

"So that's it? I don't get a choice?" Damn. I sound so angry. I'm getting loud, and there's a nasty edge to my voice. I don't even recognize it. I stand, sending the chair scraping back.

Scrap stays in his seat. When he speaks, he's completely calm. Measured. "No, you don't."

He stares at me, his elbows resting on his knees, and I can see the deep line between the hard muscles of his back, running down his spine. He's so strong. So much stronger than me.

"You know, baby, you can be angry with me." He's so fucking chill and unconcerned. I want to smack him in his chill and unconcerned face.

"I'm not angry at you." I stand and fold my arms, glaring over his head.

"You're angry. At me. The world. Inch Johnson, what he did. I understand, baby. You can be angry. I can take it. You want to hit me. I can see it. Hit me."

"I'm not going to hit you."

"Won't hurt me none." With any other man, it'd come off as arrogance, but this is Scrap Allenbach. "Let that anger out."

"I'm *not* angry." And I hadn't been. Scared, yes. Vigilant, yes. But not so pissed off at the world that I come off like a hysterical, foul-tempered bitch. Not 'til he came back.

I need him to shut up, but he keeps going. "There's nothin' you feel that I can't take. Back then...I was weak. I ain't weak no more."

I know he's not. He should be worn down. Ten years on

the inside. Bullet did eighteen months and came out born again. But Scrap...he stands tall.

"You can ask me anything you want, Crista. You can tell me anything."

My eyes are burning now, and I wish I could blink and be out of here. This is too much. I don't know what to do.

"You should let it go," I say. "It's all the past anyway."

He's silent a long time. I guess he agrees. I know I'm right, but there's a weight that makes my legs heavy as I start to walk away.

"Crista."

I stop. Turn. He's still leaning forward, but his head is raised, and those crystal blue eyes are as clear as a summer sky.

"Ain't the past. Ain't never gonna be in the past between you and me."

And I can't make out if he means that like a curse or a threat or what.

"I'm not yours. You're not mine. This isn't going to happen." I can't bear to see my words hit his face, so I give him my back and stalk off back toward the main garage.

My heart's aching like it's been squeezed in a fist, which doesn't make sense. I hardly know Scrap Allenbach, right? I kind of knew a twenty-one-year-old prospect with serious eyes, but now? I have no idea what kind of man this is, and he sure as shit doesn't know me. Why should it tear me up to tell him he's barking up the wrong tree?

I get halfway up the drive before I hear his heavy boot tread behind me. He falls into step, close but not too close.

I glance over.

He shrugs. "Gotta get some Lexus keys from up at the shop." He quirks up the corner of his mouth.

And we walk the rest of the way together.

7

SCRAP

The thing about Crista Holt is that not only did she go through what happened with Inch Johnson, even before that, she was shy as hell. I must have taken her home from band practice a half dozen times, sat next to her at cookouts and days at the lake. That whole time, she probably said ten words to me. *Thank you, Scrap. Okay, Scrap.* And she'd blush so red I was afraid Pig Iron'd think I was talking dirty to her, and he'd call chaos on my ass.

So the fact that I been sittin' at her bar for two hours now, and she's only said four words to me? It ain't out of character.

It seems to be pissin' off the sweetbutts, though. They keep hangin' on me and casting Crista looks, talkin' real loud for her benefit. I ain't Creech or Forty; I don't have that dick gene that lets you just say *git gone*. Wish I did.

All these tits in my face are causin' a great deal of hassle for me. Crista's makin' herself scarce at the other end of the bar, and I'm gettin' pissed off. I'm slammin' beers quicker than I would normally so she'll come back down and gimme a fresh one.

She's cute as hell today. She's wearin' the same light green hoodie and torn jeans from the other day, or close enough that I can't tell the difference. Her hair's tucked behind her ears. She keeps herself busy, always wipin' something down or restocking or drying mugs.

Compare her to the sweetbutt strokin' my arm, maybe she don't come off so good. The sweetbutt's big, bouncy titties are hangin' out of her skintight dress, and she's wearing stripper heels. She's tanned and tight and all the brothers at the bar are appreciating the peeks of her ass cheeks as she shifts on her stool.

She ain't got Crista's freckles, though. She ain't got the pretty red in her hair that only flashes when the sun hits it just right.

"So what do you say, Scrap? Want to take me up to your room for a real welcome home?"

Shit. How'd we get to that? Last I was payin' attention, this chick was telling me about her plans to be a Jäger-meister girl at Thunder in the Valley.

Where's Crista? Did she h—

Crack. Thump. Crista plunks a beer in front of me.

She's clenched her jaw to the point her chin has dimpled. Yeah, she heard that.

I still have over half a beer left; I don't need no refill. Guess Crista's not too keen on the direction of this conversation. I can't stop the smile.

Unfortunately, my smile is ill-timed. The sweetbutt, Angel, takes it to mean I'm open to her proposition.

"Lemme finish this and then we'll go, and I'll suck you off good. I bet you missed that upstate, didn't you?" She smooths my hair, and my skin crawls.

Crista's pulling her hands into her hoodie sleeves. Shit. I need to turn this around.

"Thank you, honey, but uh, I'm gonna finish my beer. Beers."

Angel seems to take this as a challenge. She walks her fingers down my chest, ignoring Crista. I wonder if they have beef or if Angel's just a bitch. Regardless, I'm about to not be nice about it when Crista slams a cutting board onto the counter behind the bar, and then jumps like she startled herself.

She shakes it off and grabs some limes, diving after one that she drops on the floor. Damn but that girl is always messing with limes. I didn't figure my brothers took so much fruit in their drinks, but shit has changed since I went away.

It takes her awhile scrounging under the bar to find that lost lime. I guess someone ain't as cool as she acts.

Angel rests her hand on my thigh and squeezes. "We can wait until you've finished your beer. What is it they say? Waiting makes it taste even better?"

Crista pops back up. "Hunger is the best spice," she mutters under her breath.

"True." I meet Crista's eyes in the mirror behind the bar. She's got her back to me, and she's hackin' away at those limes again. "A long wait don't make you forget. Makes you want it more."

"What I'm gonna do to you, Scrap Allenbach. You won't forget." Angel's whispering so loud, spit hits my ear.

"Just because something don't come easy, don't mean waiting is wasted time. I'm a patient man."

Tiny, rosy circles bloom on Crista's cheeks. Oh, she knows I'm talking to her. And she ain't scurrying off to the other side of the bar anymore. She's all ears.

Angel laughs. "Honey, I don't know what you're talkin' about. You're gonna cum *real* easy."

I ignore her. "For example, a man who's waiting patiently can sit back and take in the view." I stare at Crista's backside. You can't see shit between the huge hoodie and the men's jeans, but it's the thought that counts.

In the mirror, Crista rolls her eyes. I grin, and a flush creeps up her neck. That's one thing I like about her boy haircut. You can see her neck. It's real thin and graceful like a dancer or something. I want to nibble on that neck 'til she moans.

"A man could satisfy himself just watching a pretty woman."

Crista slices faster.

"The way she moves. The way she blushes so pretty."

Crista's face is flaming, now.

Angel huffs and drops her hand off my thigh. "Am I interrupting something?"

"Yup." I keep my eyes on my woman.

"I, uh, I need to get something from the back," Crista mumbles, and she bolts.

Angel watches Crista go and leans back in her stool. "Really? 'Cause it don't seem like I am interrupting."

I shake my head. "Ain't happenin', Angel."

"You're beatin' your head against a wall."

"Lucky I got a hard head."

Angel rolls her eyes and wanders away to try her luck with Wall. I wait a few minutes, polishing off one of my beers. It's pretty mellow in the clubhouse tonight. The prospects are playing pool. Creech and Hobs are shootin' the shit on a couch by the jukebox while Bucky sits between them, getting his dick sucked. Annie's flirting with Bullet in a corner, taking advantage of the fact that Pig Iron and Deb are M.I.A.

It don't escape my notice that Heavy, Forty, Charge, and Pig Iron are holed up in Heavy's office again, and I'm out here. Even Harper's back there.

I get it. Our old beef with the Rebel Raiders is flaring up again, and I'm on parole. It's penny ante shit so far—vandalism, breaking and entering—and it'd be stupid for me to have to serve out five more years over that kind of stupid shit.

Do they think if I was in the discussions, I'd go seeking it out, though? Shit. I ain't Nickel.

I tell myself to breathe. They're just tryin' to have my back. If any serious decisions are to be made, Heavy'll bring it to church. I ain't sidelined. At least that's what I tell myself as I drink beer alone at a bar with nothin' but pissed off club pussy for company.

I ain't accustomed to feeling sorry for myself. What's Crista doin' in the back anyway? She hiding in Deb's office again?

I should check. See if she needs help. Goddamn but I'm pussy whipped.

I head for the hall she disappeared down. The door to the storage room at the end is cracked open. She's probably stockin' up on more limes.

When I get closer, I can hear her rustlin' around in there. I stop in the doorway—I don't want to startle her or nothin'. She's got her back to me with a box propped on one hip, and she's reaching for a bottle on a high shelf.

"I can—" I start to offer to help, and she screams so loud I jump out of my skin. It's a horrible scream, and all my muscles leap to fight whatever it is that's scared the ever-loving-shit out of this woman.

She drops the box and glass bottles shatter. She keeps screaming, and she drops to the floor and scrabbles under the bottom shelf, shoving herself in as far in as she can get. The shelf sways, bottles fall, and the screaming won't stop.

I don't know what to do. I'm frozen in place.

She jerks her knees to her chest to protect her belly, throwing her arms over head. Footsteps come charging down the hall. I raise my fists, prepare to defend myself. I'm about to get a beating, but I don't blame 'em. If I heard this screaming, I would stomp the shit out of whatever was causin' it just to make it stop.

"Crista—" I start to tell her to not be scared, but you can't hear anything over her screams and my brothers' shouts. A half dozen of them careen to a halt behind me. I'm expecting someone to slam me into a wall at any second.

Instead, Wall hollers, "It's only Crista."

"Fuck. Again?" Creech bitches.

"I was gettin' my dick sucked." I'm about to punch Bucky's face flat when Annie elbows through the crowd and shoves past me.

"Back the fuck off, assholes. You know the drill." She sweeps aside some glass with her foot as she goes to squat next to Crista. "Crista. Crista!"

All the brothers kind of wander off back to the main room. Wall claps me on the back.

The screams trail off.

I walk closer. Crista's got herself wedged almost flush to the wall.

Annie waves a hand behind her for me to stop where I'm at. "You're in the clubhouse storage room, Crista. Let's get grounded." She snorts. "I guess you already have that covered. Let's breathe now. In and out. In and out."

There's silence, an unnerving, horrible silence, and then I hear Crista breathing. Something inside me loosens.

"Annie, is she okay?"

"What the fuck do you think?" Annie glares at me. "Why don't you go back to heavy petting Angel at the bar."

"I didn't—I didn't mean to scare her. I wasn't tryin' to sneak up or anything. Is—Is she okay?"

Annie sighs. "She'll be fine. This happens sometimes. Not so much anymore, but...It wasn't your fault. Will you fuck off now?"

"What can I do?" She's curled up so tight under there, and there's so much glass. Memories of the gas station flicker in my mind, but I tamp that shit down.

"You can fuck off." Annie looks around, finds a piece of folded cardboard, and sets it in front of her so she can kneel. She reaches out to stroke Crista's hair. "Step five, girlfriend. What do you smell?"

There's a faint mumble from under the shelves that I can't make out.

Annie huffs a laugh. "That's right. Whiskey. Smells like whiskey up in here. What do you hear?"

"Do you want me to help her out of there?" I squat so I'm on level.

"No. I want you to fuck off. *Crista* wants you to fuck off." Annie turns to face me. "Listen, I get that you care, but you need to go. She doesn't want you here. Shit, she doesn't want *me* here. Just go. She'll be fine."

I get it, and it kills me. Takes me back to that day at the SCI Wayne visiting room. The week before, when I'd gotten jumped by five lifers in the yard. The guard had been conveniently checking his watch. I spent seventy-two hours in the SHU off of that, and I wasn't thinkin' too clear when Crista came.

I remember bein' scared as shit that another inmate would figure out who she was to me, but worse than that, I couldn't stand her seeing my fucked-up face and knowing how weak I was. I didn't want to see her face when she realized that what I done didn't leave her safe. It left her alone.

When it came down to it, the shame was stronger than anything else. Took years for me to come to grips with that.

So I nod to Annie and back off. Make my way back to the main room where everyone is playin' pool or shooting darts as if nothing happened. The big meeting must have broken up cause Harper's hanging with Angel now at the bar. I go to retrieve my beer.

"She okay?" Angel asks.

I grunt.

Harper reaches over the bar and grabs herself a bottle of vodka. She sets to prying the liquor pourer from the top.

"I thought you were gonna come back and little Crista was gonna pull herself together." Harper raises an eyebrow. She's in her lawyer suit. Looks uncomfortable.

"You slumming it?" I change the subject. I've known Harper Ruth all my life. She's a bitch; you can't take it personal.

"Why? You think you're not good enough for me?" Harper tips the bottle back, doesn't even pause to swallow. Damn. "I'm not with Charge anymore. We could test it out. See where the chemistry between us leads."

"There's no chemistry." I reach behind the bar, grab a glass, and set it in front of her. She ignores it and continues to chug from the bottle. She's always been hard, but there's an edge to her now. A bitterness. "Besides, I heard you're with Des Wade, now."

Harper laughs, but it don't sound happy. "Yeah. He's slumming it, too."

"Why you so mad, Harper?" She broke things off with Charge a few months back, and he's moved on to a sweet young thing with a kid. I don't know what's goin' on—I'm nowhere near in the loop—but as I understand it, the split was her call.

"I'm fine, Scrap Allenbach. You worry about your dysfunctional girlfriend. This doesn't seem to be working out the way everyone thought it would."

"Yeah? And how did everyone think it'd go?" I fucking know better than to get pulled into her bullshit, but I've still got Crista's screams ringing in my ears, and honestly, I'm at a loss.

"I don't know. You'd come home and Crista would stop clinging so hard to being the victim. Maybe she'd throw the man who did a dime for her fat ass a bone. Look him in the eye and speak to him, maybe? Pull her head out of her ass." Harper shrugs.

I clench my fists. I know better than to take her bait, but if she was a man, she'd be missin' teeth.

"You're a cold bitch, Harper."

"I know." She pats my hand as she takes another long swig. "And you're barking up the wrong tree. There's no happy ever after back there." Harper nods toward the storage room. "Only an opportunity for you to make shit even worse. Steer clear, Scrap. Keep your nose clean. Don't make all the time I spent getting your ass out early a waste of time."

I GUESS I'm the only man in The White Van who'd rather be anywhere else. It ain't the place itself. It's nice enough for a strip club, or dark enough so that the dirt don't show.

The dancers are hot, especially Story, the blonde shakin' her ass on stage right now to "Sweet Caroline." Unusual choice for a song, but it's a crowd pleaser. Nickel's in a doorway staring at her like he wants to either eat her or cover her up, so maybe I ain't totally alone in my misery.

Hell, I really shouldn't be bitchin' considering the women are all buyin' me drinks. Still, it ain't the place I want to be.

I want to hang with my brothers, though, and it's either the clubhouse or here. And after the other night...I'm gonna need a minute to grow my balls back enough to see Crista again. And I hate to admit it, but Harper got in my head.

That picture I had in my head? Of Crista Holt in a pretty dress, snakin' her arms around me while we ride off on the back of my bike? That first night, I knew it was unlikely, but every day since drives home that I been survivin' on pure fantasy. The episode in the storage room put the last nail in the coffin.

What kept me goin' for ten years ain't nothin' but a bull-shit fairy tale I was tellin' myself to get through the day.

That's some sobering shit to come to terms with. Enough to turn you indifferent in a strip club.

"Ready for another?" Cue pours me another shot before I can answer.

This round here's gonna be on Heavy. He plopped his gargantuan ass next to mine about a few minutes ago, chasin' off the pussy. The ladies want to fuss over me since I been gone so long. It's some fuckin' shit to have all these women want you, all except the one you want.

Heavy clinks his glass against mine. "Slainte."

"If you say so, brother." I take a sip.

Heavy chuckles. "It's Irish. It means: good health."

"My health ain't my problem."

"No. Guess it's not." Heavy swings so he's facing the club, leans back with his elbows on the bar, and surveys the scene. He's always on watch, this one. Even when we was young bucks together, he always sat back and took it all in. "You want me to talk to her?"

"What would you say?" I don't like the idea. It ain't his place, but he's my president, and my brother besides. I'll hear him out before I tell him to mind his own fuckin' business.

He sighs. "I don't know, man." He keeps scanning the room, considering the naked chicks and the clientele the same. That's Heavy. So above it all he's hardly human. "I don't want you to feel like you can't hang at your own clubhouse."

"That ain't what this is."

Heavy goes on like I didn't speak. "I don't want to take the bar from her."

"Don't want you to." I wouldn't let him. Crista's safest there. I'd go nomad before I let them push her out.

"It's on me, you know. What happened back then." Heavy sniffs. It's a habit he has.

"It's was on Inch Johnson." I spit the bastard's name.

Maybe I should feel guilt for taking a man's life, but I never have. For the parole hearing, Harper had to coach me. She wrote me a script to memorize about how sorry I am for the Johnson family's loss. I could say that, I could even mean it, but there was no way I could have said I was sorry for what I done.

"Inch Johnson was getting revenge for Dutchy. Dutchy was on me." Heavy has always owned that, but I was at church when we called chaos. It was a unanimous decision.

"Dutchy took a baseball bat to Hobs' head."

"And Dutchy did it 'cause Pops got Stones and Knocker sent upstate."

Shit. It all goes back to that fuck up, don't it?

"Man, the blown job was almost twenty years ago. We were kids back then. You can't take on the burden of shit that went down way before our time."

"All I'm sayin' is Crista paid for what I did. I know this. Even if she weren't Pig Iron's kid, she'd still be Steel Bones."

It's pissin' me off, him talking about her like this. Like he can make decisions about her. Like she ain't mine. I'm shit out of ideas at the moment for how I'm gonna turn this clusterfuck around, but it don't change basic facts.

"I ain't asked you to do nothin'."

Heavy exhales, props the heel of his boot on the stool. "I know, I know. There's just been a lot of shit talk. You don't come around the clubhouse except to crash, brothers see it as Crista drove you off. Crista is family and all, but you did a dime for her. Your brothers love you. They wanna see you around. They wanna have your back."

"They don't need to."

"Some of the women. They know she freaked out at you. Gave you the cold shoulder. They think it ain't right, and they ain't known for keepin' their mouths shut. Or their hands to themselves."

"Ain't their business."

"I could find her a job here. Or I could set her up with something she could do at home. Paperwork."

"Fuck, no." The blood's rushed to my head at this point. I can feel the pulse points in my temple throb, the vein that pops when I'm getting reading to fight. "Crista ain't workin' around a bunch of dick-strokin' pervs. And as I understand, she sure as shit don't need to spend more time in her place."

Heavy raises a hand like *whoa*, but I ain't done. "And anyone who wants to talk shit can come and talk to my face. People wanna talk? I got some questions. You. Pig Iron. Nickel. Forty. Charge. Creech. Gus. Big George. Shit, even Boots came to visit me upstate. No one ever tells me Crista's fucked up?"

"She ain't fucked up."

"Bullshit. I *seen* it, brother. She got startled, and she lost her shit. And the way Annie was on it, the way the brothers reacted? That wasn't a one-off. That shit's got to be happening all the fuckin' time."

Heavy at least has the decency to look away. "Way less now than before."

"What the fuck *was* that?"

"Flashback. She had them a lot at first. Now she can go four, five months sometimes."

"Four or five months?" There's a stone in my gut. "What else? You need to tell me now, man."

"What do you want to know?"

Everything. How does he not understand this? I thought I knew. I had this picture of her happy and healthy. Fuck, I was in *love* with that picture. It got me *through*. And to find out it was bullshit?

"I'll tell you what. I'm gonna ask you the same thing I did every time you came up, and this time, you're gonna tell me the whole fucking truth. How is Crista?"

Heavy gets real still. I'll never know how a man so big and shaggy can go so motionless. He's like a mountain, kind of looms over mortal men.

"At first, it was real bad. She was in a lot of pain. She got addicted to the pain meds. Pig Iron had to wean her off the hard way."

"The hard way?"

"Cold turkey up at my cabin."

My gut knots.

"There were a few surgeries. They'd think she was all better, and something would come up. Intestinal obstructions. Shit like that. She got real skinny."

"She ain't skinny now."

Heavy raises an eyebrow.

"It ain't a complaint." It's not. I love how she can't hide her curves, even though she tries.

"She got agoraphobic for a while. She'd only leave the house with Deb or Pig Iron. Then, as Deb tells it, one day they stop for gas on the way back from a doctor's appointment, she flips the fuck out, and then after that, she says she wants a gun."

"What set her off?"

Heavy shrugs. "Who could say? Pig Iron took her up to Liberty Arms."

I nod. Nice choice. "What he get her?"

"A Beretta."

"An M9?"

"A Nano. Better for concealed carry."

"Somebody taught her how to shoot?"

"Deb did. Out back of the clubhouse."

"She a good shot?"

"Almost as good as Deb."

"And you couldn't tell me all this?"

Heavy sighs. "It was like one step forward, one step back. Pig Iron gets her moved into the apartment above his garage, and she don't come out for a month. She starts workin' the bar, she beats the shit out of a hang around. Pulls a knife on him. She was gonna do him, too. Right there on the floor. Wall had to haul her off his ass."

"What'd the guy do?"

"He was drunk, and he bumped into her on the way to the john. Ran his mouth before he thought better of it. The whole club heard."

"She beat the shit out of him?"

"Not like we weren't gonna back her play. She's Steel Bones. He was a fuckin' hang around." Heavy shrugs. "I guess we was thinkin' it might help her work some shit out."

"Did it?"

"I mean, not really, but it saved us the mistake of makin' the guy a prospect. He had fifty pounds on her, and he couldn't handle himself worth shit."

"Why didn't you tell me this shit?"

"We told you about her."

I shake my head. "Big George, when he come up, he always told me about her car. First how she was tryin' to decide between a Charger and a Mustang. You know we talked the whole time during visiting hour about whether eight more horsepower makes a fuckin' difference?"

"I would've gotten the Charger."

"Me, too, but apparently George got a deal on a pre-owned GT that she liked."

Heavy blinks, waitin' for me to get to the point.

"Every time George visits, he's tellin' me about that Mustang, and all the things he's tellin' her to do with it, and how she don't care about nothin' except steering wheel covers and vanity tag holders."

I shake my head, knock my glass on the bar for a refill.

"Ten years of talkin' about cars, and not once did he mention that Crista's too scared to drive anywhere but home and work."

"No one wanted to make it harder on you."

"How about Charge? That fucker was up there every week when he wasn't locked up himself. He told me the color of every fuckin' tile and countertop and wall and carpet in that fancy mansion Harper bought, but he couldn't mention that Crista Holt's apparently been wearin' the same hoodie and jeans day after day?"

"I think she's got a few pairs. Ain't just the one."

I want to be pissed. I want to get mad enough to fight, but it's all so fucking sad.

"I don't know what to do, man. I know it's my own fault. I told her don't come up. I was happy to let you all bullshit me. But what do I do now?"

"She ain't the same, man. No one would be after what she went through."

"She still mine. However she is now."

Heavy lays his hand on my shoulder, and the pressure is love and regret. "I don't think she can be, my brother."

I can hear that he means his words. My stomach sours.

"We got to figure out a way to move forward. You belong at the clubhouse. So does she. And the shit talk ain't gonna help the situation none. Deb's gonna end up crackin' a sweetbutt's skull."

"That's an easy solution. Someone says shit, send them my way."

"You gonna take the sweetbutts out back to the fire ring and go twelve rounds?"

"Shit. I ain't lastin' no twelve rounds against no sweet-butt and you know it. Them bitches are brutal."

"That they are, my brother." Heavy cracks a smile and slaps the bar for a beer.

"I'll be back around. I'm just bein' a pussy for a while."

"Well, I guess you fit in here."

"Guess I do." We clink glasses. "Slanted."

"Slainte." Heavy's rumbling laugh fills the air, and I roll my shoulders. This ain't hopeless.

Starin' down a fifteen-year stretch? That'll suck the hope right out of you. Lived through that, got out in ten. It's only been a month dancin' around Crista Holt. It takes a few more months, a year or two?

I got nothin' but time, and I'm used to doin' time.

8

CRISTA

Well, I guess whatever's between Scrap and me *is* in the past. After he startled me into a premium, Grade A flashback, he hasn't showed up to the clubhouse for three weeks. At first, I thought it was because shit's been flaring up with the Rebel Raiders, and Heavy doesn't want him around where he can get pulled into shit and have his parole revoked. Then I heard Cue talkin' about how Scrap's been spending his evenings at The White Van, so I guess he's not been keeping out of trouble so much as getting into some pussy.

I get it. Ten years is a long time if you're normal.

My chest aches, but it almost feels good. Pain is familiar. I understand it, and it has a way of pushing the bullshit out of your brain.

There's plenty of bullshit, too. Everyone's blaming me for Scrap not being around. Mom and Annie are watching me even closer than usual. Dad acts like I pissed in his Cheerios. I think he had his heart set on Scrap coming back and me turning into his sweet little girl again.

I try really hard not to give a shit. I work, I go home,

read, let Frances out to run around the backyard. That's what I'm doing now, sitting on a chaise lounge out behind my place, e-reader in my lap, watching him trot to Mom and Dad's back door and then back to me. He wants a treat, but no one's home.

I got Frances when I came home after one of the surgeries. It was hitting home that I'd never be able to carry kids, and I kind of wanted to care for something other than my own health for a change. I also had this idea that a guard dog would help with the hypervigilance, so I got Frances from the shelter. He doesn't guard anything but his food dish.

It's Saturday, and Dad said he wants me to take a night off, that he'll cover the bar. He says I've been working too hard, but that's bullshit, too. I haven't been doing any more than usual. I think they want Scrap to come hang out, and they want me gone so I don't make it all awkward and piss Scrap off to the point he does nothing but spar out back with whoever's drunk and stupid enough to fight him. That's what he was doing before he stopped coming around.

I wish I was at work. I'm bored and antsy. I'm between books, and my place is clean despite Grinder's best efforts to hide all his empties and dirty drawers in random places like the world's foulest Easter Bunny.

Frances isn't exactly high maintenance. He's getting on in years, and basically, he's interested in whatever I'm interested in. Curling up on the couch? He's down with that. Laying in bed? He's down. Treats are the only thing that get him excited.

He whines at Mom and Dad's door once more before he gives up and comes to lay next to me, plopping his wrinkly head on his front paws. His tongue lolls out like he's been running for miles instead of a yard or so.

It's getting hot. I shove up my hoodie sleeves. Damn, my forearms are white.

A car purrs down Dunston Avenue. I stiffen, but it doesn't turn off on Jackson. Birds are chirping. Someone's running a hose down the street by the Aronson's.

My keys are in my pocket. The Beretta in my glove box is ten feet away. I could be in my place or Mom and Dad's in thirty seconds. Frances is snoozing by my side. I'm safe.

Why is my body wound so tight? It's a weird tight, too. More amped up than freaked out. It's not my usual anxiety and paranoia cocktail.

Maybe I should cook something. That would take some time. Distract me. I've got some kiwi fruit that haven't quite gone mushy yet. Green peppers. Frozen fish sticks. Eggs.

Yeah, cooking's out.

I swipe through the library on my e-reader. Maybe there's a book worth a reread. Or a download I forgot about.

I can't keep my eyes on the screen. I keep checking out my body. My cuticles are shredded. My boots are getting really scuffed on the toes. Laying flat like this, my thighs spread so wide they almost flub over the edges of the chaise lounge. No wonder Scrap's at The White Van. The girls there are tight.

Ugh. Why do I even care what he does?

I need to get out of my head. What do normal people do when they get bored and down on themselves? They go out.

Ain't happening.

They text a friend. I have friends. Not "go out places" friends, but there are girls I hang with at the clubhouse. Fay-Lee. Story.

Fay-Lee's always asking me to come to her house and check out the hot tub Dizzy got her. Watch TV. I think she gets lonely watching his boys. She comes from a family of,

like, twenty kids or something, so alone time freaks
her out.

I should call Fay-Lee. It's four thirty. The boys'll be
home, but Dizzy won't be home from work yet, since he
manages for Big George on Saturdays at the Autowerks. I
bet she's bored.

I pull up my Contacts. My finger hovers over the green
phone icon. Am I really going to call someone and speak to
them on the phone?

Nope.

I open the text app instead.

What r u doing?

It literally takes seven seconds, and my phone is ringing.
I'm so startled, I fumble it.

"What are *you* doing?" Fay-Lee is so loud, I don't need to
put her on speaker.

"I'm bored."

"Yes!" I can almost hear the fist pump.

I can't help but chuckle. "I'm happy that my boredom
makes you happy."

"Honey, I been waiting for you to get bored since I met
you. I'm coming over."

Whoa. That wasn't what I was thinking. I don't have
people over.

"You want me to bring a DVD?" I can hear rustling on
her end.

"What? No. What about the boys?"

"Parker's in eighth grade. He can watch his brother for a
few hours."

"Is Dizzy cool with that?"

"So what if he's not? Win-win, that's what I say."

Fay-Lee and Dizzy have a weird relationship. She started
out as his house mouse when her man bailed on her a few

years back and she got stranded at the clubhouse. Now she wears a collar and calls Dizzy "Daddy" when his kids aren't around. She lives to get him riled up.

"Well? Should I pick up some Zimas on the way over?"

"Zima? Like from the 90s?"

"It's back, baby! I'll get some Jolly Ranchers, and we'll get sloppy and all girly-girl."

"How do you even remember Zima?" I hardly remember sneak-chugging Annie's and replacing it with Sprite, and Fay-Lee's five or six years younger than me.

"You know how some moms put Benadryl in the baby's bottle to get them to go down?"

"Yeah?" This is going to be another fucked up Fay-Lee Parsons origin story.

"Well, Zima costs way less than Benadryl. A little for Roy Junior or Terrance, a lot for big sis, you know?"

"That's the worst thing I've ever heard."

"You know it's not." Fay-Lee laughs real big, and a small blossom of warmth erupts in my chest. This is why I love Fay-Lee. To her, with the things she's seen in her life? What happened to me isn't the worst thing she's ever heard of. "So that's a yes to the Zima? I'll be over in an hour."

"Okay?"

She's hung up already.

Frances snuffles and rolls over on his side. His tongue flops as he rolls.

It's really hot out here. I should go inside, give the place a once over. Grinder's at the clubhouse, but who knows what he left out. At a minimum, I should shut his door so no one can see the wreckage. Ernestine's a saint for only putting that man out every few years.

I can't bring myself to move, though. The sun's kind of

soothing on my face. I unzip my hoodie, shrug it down my shoulders. The warmth feels good on my neck and chest.

My feet are baking in my boots. I untie them, heel them off, and roll down my socks. Damn. My feet are so freakin' white, they glow. The sun and the light breeze feel good on them, too, though. I wiggle my toes. Frances whines, plops his head on the bottom of the chaise lounge, and starts sniffing.

"You want to lick my toes, you have to buy me dinner first."

Frances gives me a lazy side-eye before he snorts and drifts off, again.

The sky's a perfect blue today.

I want to see Scrap.

The urge comes from nowhere, but it settles in my stomach, and I squirm.

I want to see him.

I don't want all the heavy shit, the whispers and gossip and panic and memories. I just want to watch him like he was in the hangar, his shirt hanging out of his back pocket, a small band of his plaid boxers visible above the waist of his jeans. His stance, so easy, but so ready at the same time. Like he owned the space.

I felt frumpy next to him. Squat. Awkward. But breathless, too. Not afraid for once.

Excited.

That's the thrum that's making me so restless. It's so close to fear, maybe I got mixed up. I lay here, soaking up the sun, and I let my mind wander to him, stalking toward me in the clubhouse that first day, his stride so confident, that half-smile gentling his sternness.

My stomach bubbles, but not in a bad way. More champagne than nausea.

I'm drifting and daydreaming for maybe an hour when the buzz of an engine turning onto Jackson yanks me from my thoughts. I spring up, grab my phone, and zip my hoodie back up. By the time Fay-Lee's Jeep pulls into the drive, I'm tugging on my socks.

To my surprise, a short woman with a dark halo of wild, curly hair pops from the passenger seat. It's Nevaeh Ellis. Her brother, Lou, is a hang around, and she used to date Forty in high school. She dropped out of school and left for Pyle when Forty joined the service. Now she's back. Petty's Mill is like that. People turn back up like a bad penny.

My mind careens for a second to man pumping gas, but I drag it back into the moment. Nevaeh is a great distraction. She's a lot to take, kind of a cross between an 80's hair band groupie and a barker at a carnival who really wants you to win a goldfish.

Fay-Lee works her way out of the Jeep ass first, arms full of brown bags and a purse and a tote with a beach umbrella decal...and a duffle bag?

Wow. That's a lot of crazy that just rolled up.

"Hey." I finish tying my boots.

"I'm so stoked!" Nevaeh throws her hands in the air, smacks kisses on my cheeks, and then collapses down on the grass to scratch Frances. For a short girl, all her movements are huge. Dramatic.

"Why are you stoked?" I am so afraid to ask.

"We're going out!" Nevaeh announces as if someone won a car. Shit, like *everyone* won a car. I swear Frances rolls his eyes.

"Where are you going?"

Fay-Lee has joined us, having dumped everything but a six-pack by the stairs to my place. "Jesus, Nevaeh. We're supposed to ease her into it."

"Into what?" I take the bottle Fay-Lee offers and take a long swig. I think I'm gonna need it.

"It's Saturday night, baby! We're going out." Nevaeh says this like it's good news.

"I don't go out."

"Yet. Until tonight." Fay-Lee plops down next to me. "Tonight, you go out."

"We're gonna change your life." Nevaeh's disappointed that Frances is just kind of laying there, so she starts playing with his paws like he's a marionette. She doesn't know who she's dealing with. Frances flumps flatter. It takes more than high energy to get that dog jazzed. It takes treats.

"I'm good. You guys have fun."

"Crista." Fay-Lee nudges me with her bony shoulder. "We all know that's not true."

I raise an eyebrow.

"You made the call for help. Help has arrived. Now this is how it's gonna go. I brought some cute dresses."

"Your clothes will never fit me." Fay-Lee's long and lanky. Maybe a size six. I'm a one-size-fits-all.

"They're not mine. Dizzy's ex left them."

"I don't want to wear Diane Jones' hand-me-downs."

"Don't worry. I washed them. And crabs can't swim."

"Crabs can definitely swim. They're—like—seafood." This is from Nevaeh who's folding Frances' paws on top his head and watching them slowly slide back down.

Fay-Lee and I pause a moment, blinking at each other, before Fay-Lee continues. "They're all brand name. Only the best for Diane Jones."

Before she bailed on her kids, Diane Jones only came around the clubhouse if she was looking for Dizzy to tear him a new one. I really don't want to wear her clothes. Crabs or not.

"I have a dress, but I'm not gonna wear it."

"Yes! We're going out!" Nevaeh stomps her feet and pumps her arms, and Frances slowly eyes her and then ponderously rolls to his side, giving her his back. "Is your dog seriously telling me to tone it down?"

I shrug.

Nevaeh leans over Frances, lifts one of his ears, and says, "Are you telling me to tone it down, buster?" Frances farts. Nevaeh shrieks and fans his butt.

"I can't believe you actually agreed!" Fay-Lee crows, ignoring Nevaeh.

My stomach starts to swish. I did agree to go out. How did that happen?

"Where are we going?" The first tendrils of panic creeps into my chest. What did I agree to?

"Sawdust on the Floor. It's line dancing night."

"I don't know how to line dance."

"No worries. They have a guy who calls out what to do."

"Like do-si-do, now circle left?" To be honest, that does not sound like a scene Fay-Lee or Nevaeh would be into.

"Not quite that bad. But close."

"I don't know...maybe we could go to the movies?"

"The movies isn't *out*. Besides, it's ten-dollar bottomless pitchers of beer all night long, so you're gonna have to deal with swingin' your partner round-and-round."

"Ten-dollar pitchers?"

"It's watery as shit and tastes like piss, but Dizzy has real trouble counting my drinks when there's dozens of half-full plastic cups on a table and a bottomless pitcher."

"He counts your drinks?" Nevaeh looks horrified.

"Yeah." Fay-Lee grins all wicked. "I'm allowed one per hour, three total per evening. If I have too many, I get a spanking." She says spanking like Annie says *special surprise* when she's trying to bribe my nieces.

Nevaeh relaxes. "Is this one of you guy's kinky sex things?"

"Yup." Fay-Lee makes the *p* sound pop.

"So basically, we're going line dancing so you can drink too much and drive your old man to spank you?" I just wanna be clear.

Fay-Lee considers. "Well, when you put it like that...yeah?"

Weirdly, this makes me feel a little better. This isn't all about me. Maybe it's not even mostly about me. My anxiety eases a bit. "Is he meeting us there?"

"Not quite. I've got a scheme."

"So who's driving? I can drive." Sawdust on the Floor is on the way to the clubhouse, right before Main Street turns into Route 9. My brain runs the route.

"I'm driving," Fay-Lee counters.

"No, you're not. You're drinking."

"Exactly. I'm gonna have to call Dizzy to come drive us home."

"I feel weird being part of your kinky sex games."

"Not me." Nevaeh rolls onto her stomach and kicks her legs up, back and forth. "I love being part of your kinky sex games. I'm gonna be the bad influence."

"No, your job is to take lots of pics and post them on social media. I bet Dizzy shows up twenty minutes after the first pic of me with a beer in my hand."

"Do I get a job?" I ask.

"You've already done it." Fay-Lee pats my thigh and stands.

"Yeah?"

"Why do you think Dizzy even agreed to let me go out

dancing at a bar without him? With Nevaeh Ellis, for heaven's sake?" She glances at Nevaeh, but there has been no offense taken. "I told him we were helping you work through your trauma, and you needed a girl's night to, like, heal or some shit."

"It was very compelling bullshit." Nevaeh's nodding, her brown eyes rounded.

"Are you guys serious?"

"As serious as we ever are."

I really have no idea what to think. Talking to these two is like taking Frances to the vet when it's busy. There's so much yapping and random movement that I'm kind of overwhelmed.

I'm not panicking, though. I think I'm about to move the perimeter of my life, and instead of being terrified, I'm kind of...amused.

"Okay. I should get ready."

"I'm doing your makeup!" Fay-Lee pulls an enormous Caboodle from her duffle bag.

"Dibs on hair!" Nevaeh pops to her feet, and the mop on her head springs up and down a few times.

I'm shaking my head as they circle me like hyenas. "I got it covered, ladies."

It takes about five times longer than it should to get ready to go. I'd thrown on a clean hoodie and jeans in a minute, but I didn't figure that when I turned down a makeover, Fay-Lee and Nevaeh would decide to do each other up instead.

They crowded me at the bathroom mirror while I brushed my teeth, and then trailed after me into my bedroom, asking me what I thought about this eyeshadow or that hair style.

It was hectic and awkward and kind of nice. It reminded

me of way back in the day when Annie would be getting ready for a date, and she'd let me play in her makeup and help her pick her outfits.

Fay-Lee kept a Zima in my hand, and Nevaeh blasted music, bounding around the place, hopping on the sofa to dance, generally driving Frances nuts. You could tell by the way he occasionally opened one eye to glare at her.

Whenever my anxiety would surge, I'd get distracted, so it wasn't until the car ride that my nerves really started riding me.

It's only a fifteen-minute drive to the bar, a route I take every day, but it all looks different tonight. Stark. Somehow more real, like the world's in HD. When we pass the gas station across from Finnegan's ice cream, I make myself look. There's no man working the pumps. The bay doors of the garage are closed for the night.

I don't blink, and I don't let myself look away. Soon enough, it's in the rearview.

I try to relax, but I can't get comfortable. The jeans I had clean are tighter than my usual, and the button is digging into my middle.

"How you doin' back there?" Fay-Lee calls as she pulls into the parking lot beside the bar. It's well lit, and there are people hanging out and smoking, but I can't lie. My pulse is racing, and I'm nauseous as hell.

"Good. Fine."

Nevaeh flounces around to face me. "You're freakin' the fuck out, aren't you?"

I bark a laugh, and it sounds crazy. "Yes. So much."

"Me too." Fay-Lee engages the parking brake, and my heart flips.

"Why are you freaking out?" Fuck. Is there something to

worry about? I scan the parking lot, but I don't see anything. Damn I wish I had my knife. Or the Beretta.

"If this goes south, Deb and Annie are gonna beat my *ass*." Fay-Lee catches my eye in the rearview.

"And Shirlene, and Ernestine—" Nevaeh adds.

Fay-Lee shivers. "Ernestine ain't nothin' to fuck with."

"Guys. I'm fine. I'll be fine." I force myself to drag in a deep breath and push open the car door.

"I can't believe she's doing this," Nevaeh stage whispers to Fay-Lee as they get out and take position on either side of me.

"I'm the Crista-charmer." Fay-Lee walks toward the bar with way too much swagger for a girl on loose gravel in six-inch heels.

I let them pull me along between them, their elbows hooked in mine. It feels so strange. The touching. I'm not used to it. Only Annie and Mom think nothing of putting their hands on me. Everyone else keeps an extra half step away.

As we approach the propped-open door, heat and music and loud voices spill out. I know all about Sawdust on the Floor, of course. It's a Petty's Mill institution. Annie was sneaking in on a fake ID when she was in middle school. It's everything I imagined.

There's no literal sawdust, but almost. The floor is raw wood, and it creaks under your shoes. The place reeks of sour beer and sweat, but for some reason, the lights are crazy bright. The joint is huge, but still, it's busting at the seams. Every bar stool is taken, and the tables around the dance floor are crowded with people of all ages, women sitting on their men's laps, loud-talking and carrying on.

There's a man in a black cowboy hat and silver bolo tie standing on a narrow stage, bellowing "rock right" and "bump hips" on a microphone, and five or six rows of dancers.

I scan every face, and I see Roosevelt, one of the prospects, and a couple girls from The White Van. There are several more familiar faces, and some stares, of course, but it's okay.

I'm sweating, and my heart's thumping, but it's manageable. Normal-level freak out.

Fay-Lee guides me to a table with a few empty chairs, pushes me to sit, and waves Nevaeh off to get a pitcher. It's all older couples at the table, and they strike up a conversation with Fay-Lee, leaving me to check the exit points and focus on my breathing.

Maybe Fay-Lee is some kind of miracle worker 'cause I'm doing fine. I can see the rear exit down the hall to the bathrooms. It's propped open to let a breeze in. The place is hot as hell. I should take off my hoodie. I finger the cuffs. No. Hoodie stays on.

The song ends and another, slower one begins. The dancers shift into a circle and pick partners. The man with the microphone falls silent. The couples sweep by where I sit, and I watch them awhile.

There are couples my parents' age and older, some mooning at each other, some staring off into the distance, bored. Younger couples dance by, stiff and serious. Some guys cut up, twirling their girls out-of-step or copping a feel, while others keep their eyes on their feet. That'd be me, if I were out there.

A hollow longing fills my chest, edging out the nerves.

I kind of want to dance. I can't, though. My boots are too heavy, and my body's too lumpy and dumb.

"Say cheers!" Fay-Lee knocks me out of my funk by slinging her arm around my neck and posing for Nevaeh.

She's holding up a plastic cup of beer with a huge, frothy head. Girl can't pour worth shit. "Do I look cute?"

Nevaeh considers. "You're alright."

"Then post it!"

"Posted." Nevaeh taps her phone. "Five bucks your old man is here within the next five songs."

"I'll take that action." Fay-Lee chugs the beer and then crinkles the cup. "Come on, Crista Holt. Let's shake our sweet thangs."

The dancers are forming lines again, and Fay-Lee grabs my arm and leans back like a cowboy trying to get a mule to budge. Bad news for her that I outweigh and out-stubborn her.

"Maybe later. I want to watch."

Fay-Lee really leans into it. She's at an almost thirty-degree angle.

"Seriously. Let me just watch for a while."

Nevaeh intercedes, prying Fay-Lee off. "No means no, girlfriend. Come on. We'll circle back for her once she's got some liquid courage."

Fay-Lee looks ready to sit back down, so I reach to pour myself a beer. "Go on. Show me how it's done."

"You'll be okay here by yourself?"

I dart a quick glance to the elderly couples at our table. "I think I'll be all right."

"Girl, come on!" Nevaeh tugs Fay-Lee. "That man of yours is gonna be here to ruin our fun in no time. We need to seize the day!"

"You'll be fine?"

"I'll be right here."

With one last nervous glance, Fay-Lee lets herself be dragged to the dance floor, and a minute later, she's lost in laughing and shaking her ass. Fay-Lee dances really gracefully; she's a fish in water on the dance floor. Nevaeh's a trip. Every "rock right" and "bump hips" is damn near pornographic. Every man in the five lines behind her loses the beat each time the dude in the bolo tie calls a step that requires shaking your ass.

I sip my beer, and settle in to watch. It's not bad. The vibe is different from the clubhouse. No one seems here to fight or fuck, and the drunken stumbles and spills all seem to end in laughter. A low thrum of hypervigilance keeps my muscles tight, and I'm constantly scanning faces, but I'm far from freaking out. The wide-open route to the back exit really helps, as do all the chill couples.

I pour myself a second beer, and the others at my table abandon me when "Louisiana Saturday Night" comes on. It's clearly a popular tune with the senior set although Fay-Lee and Nevaeh are still going strong. Everything is mellow and fine when the mood in the place suddenly shifts hard.

There's a rustling coming from the front, a kind of displacement wave of people backing up, accompanied by raised whispers. Then, the commotion is followed by a hush underscored by the shrieks and chatter of people further into the bar who haven't yet noticed whatever just walked in.

Trouble. My mouth goes dry, and I push my chair back from the table.

I need to run.

But that's stupid. There's no reason to run. Yet. But I have a clear path if I need to. My heart eases out of my throat.

Then I see who it is, and it's so hard not to laugh.

I guess I never see civilians react to Steel Bones. I'm always at the clubhouse or the other businesses where it's nothing to see a bunch of brothers hanging out. Besides, I've known all the guys for years, some for my entire life.

So from where I sit, I'm seeing Heavy, Dizzy, Forty,

Nickel, Creech, Wall, a few prospects, and—oh, shit—Scrap walk into a bar.

Everyone else must be seeing zombie Vikings descending on their peaceful village. People give the guys a wide berth, going to ridiculous lengths to give them space. The men avert their eyes. The women gawk or blush or stare anywhere else. The man in the bolo tie forgets to call the steps.

Heavy sees me and jerks his chin toward my table. The brothers follow—all but Dizzy who's making a beeline for Fay-Lee—and there's no elbowing through the crowd. The dancers literally peel off into another row to make room for the guys to pass.

I guess I understand it. Despite the hokey soundtrack, the moment has the feel of a scene from a movie where the mild-mannered hero gulps *Oh shit.* Not one of the brothers is shorter than six feet or less than two hundred-some pounds. There's so much leather, beards, and body modification that your eyes don't know what to take in first.

Creech's tattooed head? Heavy's wild and kinky black hair? The scars and burns that decorate Forty's right arm, or the full sleeve that covers his left, including the demon cat devouring the human heart?

It's a lot if it's not your everyday.

"Crista." Heavy inclines his head and then eyes the empty chairs at the table. "These taken?"

"They were, but I think they're free now."

The brothers all sit down with a collective creaking of cheap metal folding chairs, and that seems to thaw the frozen room. Chatter slowly returns to normal although we're still the table everyone's sneaking peeks at from the corner of their eyes.

A part of me relaxes, quits scanning the crowd.

Scrap takes the seat next to mine. He's so close, I can smell his fabric softener. I swallow, but it sticks, and I cough. I take a deep sip of my beer.

Scrap grabs a plastic cup from the stack they gave us with the pitcher, pours himself a beer, and then he tops me off.

"Wash! Bush! Grab us—" Creech takes a second to count. "Eight pitchers."

"They're bottomless pitchers, man." I'm just letting him know.

"We'll see about that." Creech mutters as if this is a personal challenge.

"You havin' fun?" Scrap murmurs, resting his arm on the back of my chair. Oh my God. He's even closer now. I force myself to breathe. He isn't touching me. Not when I scooch a bit forward.

Scrap turns himself so his back is to his brothers. He's totally focused on me. His knee is brushing my thigh. I can't feel it through my jeans, but there's a pressure.

My heart stutters.

"It looked like you girls were having a good time in the pic Dizzy showed us."

I nod.

"You dance?"

I shake my head.

"You gonna talk to me, or you still mad I set you off in the storage room?"

My eyes fly up to his. His tone is light, and his expression matches. He's not pissed. His blue eyes are so light against his dark gray shirt and black cut, you could see anything in them clear as day. They're almost sparkling. He's in a good mood.

"You didn't set me off."

"I was there, Crista." He raises an eyebrow.

My face flushes. "I'm not mad, anyway."

"Why aren't you dancin'?" He changes the subject, and I can breathe a little easier.

"I don't know the steps. I've never been here before."

"Me neither."

"No?" I'm surprised. There aren't that many bars in Petty's Mill.

"When it ain't line dancing night or karaoke, it's a pickup bar. Before I went away, I wasn't into picking up women."

"Oh?" It comes out almost a squeak. I'm feeling really squirmy, which sucks, 'cause if I move at all I'll nudge into Scrap.

"I knew what I wanted. Didn't need to go lookin' for something else."

He means me. When I was sixteen. And skinny. And a functional human. My stomach wobbles. Is that a good feeling? I can't even tell.

I don't know what to say, so I take a long sip of beer.

Scrap presses his leg more firmly against mine. It'd feel like crowding if he didn't also lean back in his chair and move the arm that was around me to rest on the table. He shoots me that wry half-smile.

"I'll do it, if you do it."

"What?"

"Dance." He jerks his head at the dance floor.

"No, thank you." There's no way I'm going to jiggle my awkward ass in front of Scrap Allenbach. Grapevine left. Grapevine right. I've embarrassed myself enough in front of him since he's been back.

"You don't want to ruin your friend's good time, do you?"

What does he mean?

"Dizzy's about to haul Fay-Lee home, and if you're not dancing, that means Nevaeh will have to leave."

"Why would she have to leave?"

Scrap's smile widens. "You mean I finally know some gossip that one of ya'll don't?"

He jerks his chin at Forty who's downright glowering in the corner, arms folded so tight his huge biceps are swollen into freakin' cantaloupes.

"Him and Nevaeh hate each other. If Fay-Lee gets dragged home and you're over here with him, she'll bail."

I check out Nevaeh. She's still bumping and grinding like there's dollar bills in it for her, but now that Scrap said something, I see her sneaking looks at Forty. The more uptight he gets, the bigger her smiles are for the guys beside her in the line.

I'm not sure where Dizzy got to with Fay-Lee. Nevaeh catches me watching her, though, and she waves me over. A song has ended, and there's a general shuffling and movement on and off the floor.

Tiny bubbles flit and pop in my belly. That's excitement. What I'm feeling is excitement. It's so unfamiliar, but I kind of remember it from before.

I'm not going to dance, though. That's crazy.

Scrap scrapes his chair back and stands, holding his hand out to me. I shake my head.

"You came this far, baby. Dance floor's only a few feet further."

I blame the *baby*. How serious and soft it was. How *personal*. It throws me, and before I can think, Scrap's wrapped his big, rough hand around mine, and he's leading me to Neveah. When she sees us coming, she hollers and jumps like a drunk cheerleader.

I don't have time to panic before the music starts, and

everyone starts slapping their thighs and clapping, and then my goodness, there's so much step-twist-stomp-hold, and then there's a turn, and more stomping, and more turning, and Neveah's hollering, "Look at my feet! Look at my feet!"

I don't know what she thinks I'm doing 'cause if I stop looking at her feet for a second, I'm facing the wrong direction.

About halfway through I catch up enough to check out Scrap, and then I can't stop grinning. I've never seen a man more intent on his business. He's nailing each rock forward, each slide and touch. And by nailing I mean like a hammer does. This is less dancing and more stomping. The floor's shaking, and I'm sure it's ninety-five percent Scrap Allenbach.

I lose my place, and I guess he notices, 'cause he loses his, too. We both stand there as the song ends, gasping, grinning like idiots.

"I kicked that thing's fuckin' ass." Scrap slams down the last few steps, and before I can shove my hands in my hoodie pockets or ease away back to the table, he grabs me. "One more."

"Now grab your girls, fellas." The man in the bolo tie reaches down to hand up a silver-haired woman wearing a flouncy jean skirt. He sets down his mic and spins the woman into his arms.

Nevaeh grins at me and partners up with one of the guys she's been flirting with.

I look at Scrap. His lip quirks up.

I should sit down. "I don't know what I'm doing." It's loud as the music begins, and my voice is soft, but he hears me.

"Me neither. I won't let it go bad."

"You can't help it."

"Trust me." He pulls me into his arms, placing my hand on his shoulder. Then he checks the couples around us and puts his hand high on my back.

There's no way I can move my feet.

A man's touching me.

He's touching me. Scrap Allenbach is touching me.

My heart races. I'm so hot, and my legs feel so damn weak.

Scrap moves forward, and I shuffle back. He's not worried about the steps now; he's not staring at anyone's feet. His eyes are on me, and he's slowly closing his arms until his chest grazes my cheek.

He's swaying, and I'm swaying, too, held up by his hand on my back, and the heat and largeness of him at my front. He bends his head to my ear.

"You smell so fuckin' good. Like strawberries." His breath sends tiny shivers down my neck.

"It's my bodywash."

He sighs and straightens, and more of him is even closer now. He's rearranged my arm, folding it up behind me into the small of my back, easing me tighter to him.

I should be panicking, but I'm out-of-body, lost in his smell and the warmth of his chest.

He lifts a hand to stroke my cheek. "Your skin is so fuckin' soft."

I don't know what to say. I'm so used to my body and my brain going nuts, but they're muffled here, in this weird place out-of-time, and all I can pay attention to is Scrap. How his breathing is quicker now than when he was stomping. How his muscles are tense, but his touch is so very, very light.

"It's my bodywash," I finally mumble into the leather of his cut.

"That's some miraculous shit, ain't it? They oughta bottle it."

The giggle's out before I realize it. "Was that a joke?"

"Not if you can't tell it was." And then he dips his head down and brushes his lips across mine. I suck in a breath, almost gasp on it. Almost. He kissed me. A second ago, he kissed me, and now I can't even remember what it felt like.

"Scrap." It sounds like a plea.

He kisses me again, lingering this time, and there's more pressure, but not too much.

"I love it when you say my name," he says against my lips. "That night I came home, and you said 'hi, Scrap.' Sweetest sound I ever heard."

I stiffen a little at the memory. "I was a bitch that night."

"Your eyes were so big I could see myself in 'em. So damn pretty."

"You're so full of it."

He drops a handful of soft kisses across my cheeks, my nose, sending shivers radiating down my body, skittering from nerve to nerve, and I can't help it, I have to lean on him a little to keep myself up straight.

"What did you think? When you saw me that night?" His voice is so close to my ear. I can't pretend I don't hear the longing.

A bitter taste fills my mouth. He wants so bad for me to be what I'm not. Normal. What I was before.

What did I think? That he was older. Bigger. That I wanted to be anywhere else but there.

I could tell him the truth. Hurt him. Maybe finally convince him to give this up. Let me go back to getting along. Banish all these confusing feelings and sensations.

But.

He's holding me in this moment, but it doesn't feel that

way. It feels like I have him in my arms. And maybe I'm not strong, but I can't drop him.

"I thought you were so tall."

"I am that." He shifts me back and forth, with me wedged between his long legs, and I can tell that wasn't quite what he wanted to hear. My heart twinges. "The song's almost over."

"Yeah?" I tune in. The song is fading.

"Let me take you home, Crista."

The implications hit me like a Mack truck. I stiffen so quick I knock Scrap back a step. He doesn't let go, though.

"No, baby. Not like that. Let me ride you home. I'll walk you to your door. Say goodnight. That's all."

"Why?"

For a minute he seems mad, but then I guess he breathes, and his calm is back. It unknots something in my chest.

"I want a little longer with your arms around me. That's all."

My insides melt and those bubbles fizz in my belly.

I think I want that, too. I nod into his chest, and he groans. Then he grabs my hand and leads me off the dance floor. I look for Nevaeh, and she's already waving at me, blowing a kiss.

I'm really doing this. A shaking takes root in my core, and I stumble. Scrap tucks me into his side.

"It's just a ride, baby. Won't be the first time."

He leads me outside where there's a row of bikes backed in. His Street Bob is first in line, the same one he used to pick me up from band practice. Someone must've given it a new paint job cause it's matte now, and the chrome is spotless. There's a new decal on the gas tank, too. A Steel Bones skull and hammer and an X. The number ten.

For the years he spent in lock up. Because of me. I slam to a halt, and Scrap's grip pulls our arms taut.

"What's wrong, baby?"

He follows my line of sight and sighs.

"Yeah. Big George added the decal. He took care of her for me while I was gone. Rode her to keep her in good condition."

"I think I want to go back inside."

Scrap turns, puts his body between me and the bike. He takes both my hands, but he holds them loose at my side.

"Talk to me."

I blink up at him. I *can't*. It's all too big, too much. I can't be a girl going for a ride with some guy. I can never be a girl again, and he can never be some guy.

What happened is always there, thickening the air, waiting to suffocate me.

Scrap exhales. He drops my hands, runs his fingers through his hair. He stares up at the dark sky for a long moment, frowns, and then he skewers me with his gaze, the gentleness gone, replaced by something I haven't seen before.

"You know I would never hurt you."

I nod. I do know that.

"Say it. Say you know I'd never hurt you."

I don't know where he's going with this, but it's the least I can give him. "I know you'd never hurt me."

"Okay. Keep that in mind." Then he reaches down, wraps his arms around my thighs, and lifts me up, slinging me over his shoulder. The air goes out of my lungs in an oof.

It's so quick, I can't even scream. One second I'm dangling upside down staring at gravel, the next I'm on the back of his bike.

"Stay put," he says.

I'm so stunned I don't know what to do, so I sit there while he pulls a half shell from his saddle bag and sets it on my head.

"Can you buckle it?"

Can I—

He takes the straps and tightens them around my chin. Then he drops another kiss on my lips and mounts the bike in front of me, toeing up the kickstand.

"You can hold on to me or the back bar, but you need to pick one or the other, or I'm gonna pick for you."

He faces front, and I think my muscle memory kicks in. I wrap my arms around his middle. He spins off, pulling onto Route 9.

Oh, Lord. I *remember* this.

I remember being sixteen and riding behind Scrap Allenbach, my heart slamming against my ribs. I was so afraid he'd know how I felt—and him knowing was the worst thing that could ever happen—so I tried to barely hold him and keep my legs wide so that my thighs didn't touch his. God, my hip sockets would ache by the time we got home. And I'd lean back until my abs shook so I wouldn't be pressing my boobs against his back.

It's the same bike, but I'm a bigger woman now. There's no way I can't smoosh against him. My inner thighs cradle his hips. My boobs are crushed against his back. My arms, though, don't reach nearly so far. He's bigger now, too.

He keeps a safe speed through town, and it's a short drive. We're pulling up in my drive before I can really wrap my brain around the fact that Scrap Allenbach cave-manned me onto his bike.

He dismounts, helping me off. I unbuckle the helmet and hand it to him. I expect it to get awkward now. There'll be hemming and hawing. Maybe I'll lose my shit and get weirdly aggressive again.

He stows the helmet and heads up to my place.

He stops halfway up the stairs. "You comin'?"

Am I—? I guess I am. I follow him, unlock the door, and hold it open for him. It feels nice to let someone go first. The apartment is quiet. Grinder must be at the clubhouse. He's left five empties and a half-eaten moon pie on the coffee table.

Scrap raises an eyebrow. "Party for one?"

"Grinder." I roll my eyes. "Do you want, uh, a beer or something?"

"Sure. Anything you got."

I make my way to the kitchen, checking on my way down the hall. The utility closet's clear. Bedrooms are both clear. Bathroom is clear. Frances is in my bedroom, sleeping on a hoodie that didn't quite make it into the hamper. He gives me a sleepy blink and goes back to drooling on the carpet.

"Beer's usually in the fridge," Scrap calls from the living room. He's made himself comfortable on the sofa.

Smartass.

I'm not going to feel embarrassed. Plenty of people check the place out when they get home, people with less of a reason to do so than me.

"Sam Adams okay?" I call from the hall.

"I'm not particular."

I check the kitchen pantry, and then I bring two beers to the living room. I hand him one and sit in Grinder's easy chair.

"Am I gonna have to come over there and haul your ass over here again?"

I snort. "Yeah. What *was* that earlier? You seriously

swung me over your shoulder. You're lucky you didn't put your back out."

"That was me decidin' we ain't waitin' on your hang ups no more."

I kind of sputter. This isn't like the Scrap I've gotten accustomed to since he's been back, gentle and patient.

"I need to count to three, baby? Get your ass over here."

I don't know why I do it. Maybe because doing what he asks is easier than dealing with the garbage in my head. I go sit on the sofa, on the end.

He grabs my feet, pulls them up into his lap, and starts working on the laces.

I gasp. "What are you doing?"

"Takin' your ugly man boots off."

"Why?"

"We're gonna hang out on this sofa and watch a movie, and that ain't gonna happen if you're wearing construction worker boots."

I notice for the first time that he's taken his own shoes and socks off. His feet are bare. My stomach goes flippy, and it's so distractingly weird, him barefoot in my house, that I let him pull off my boots and roll down my socks.

Oh, please Lord, don't let my feet be stinky. I didn't dance that much.

I tense up even more, although I'm not sure how that's even humanly possible. Scrap grabs the blanket folded on the back of the sofa and covers me from my waist to my bare feet resting in his lap. Then he grabs the remote.

"What do you wanna watch?"

"I have a choice?"

"*The Fast and the Furious* it is."

"Hey—"

Scrap reaches under the blanket to tickle the bottom of

my foot, and it's so unexpected, I squeak like one of Frances' toys.

He chuckles. "That's so fuckin' cute. Do that again." And he tickles my other foot.

"Cut it out." I dig my heels into his lap, and he raises his hands.

"Peace, woman. No need to kick me in the balls. We can watch—" He thinks a minute. "What do chicks watch now?"

It's a reminder of those missing ten years, and part of me braces, getting ready to feel the weight, but the larger part of me is too enthralled by what's happening now. I'm hanging out with a man, in my apartment, snuggling on the sofa, about to watch a movie. I've seen it on TV a thousand times, but I never thought I'd be doing it.

So I answer the question. "*The Fate of the Furious*. We can rent it off Amazon."

He laughs and hands me the remote. "That's my girl."

We watch *F8*, and then we watch *Olympus Has Fallen*. I keep my feet on his lap and the blanket pulled up to my chin. At some point, he sneaks his hand under the blanket and rests it on my ankle. Then he starts stroking up my calf. My jeans won't let him go but so high.

At first, I worry that I missed a spot shaving, and I then I worry that he'll try to take my jeans off, and I'll freak out and ruin everything.

As it gets later and later and my eyes get heavier, I stop worrying. We take turns getting up to pee and fetch more beers. He says he's hungry, so I microwave some popcorn. When I hand him the bowl, he kisses me. Quick and firm.

When he finishes the popcorn, he leans over, tilts my chin, and kisses me again. This time he lingers, nibbling, licking at the seam of my lips. I open for him, because he smells like popcorn and spray butter, and Frances is snoring at our feet, and it's warm but not hot, and everything is okay, and I want to know what he tastes like.

His tongue slips inside my mouth—Scrap's tongue is in my mouth—and his stubble is chafing my chin while thousands of shivers zip up and down my spine. Between my legs, a faint aching starts. I feel floaty and punch drunk, but not at all tired, and I think I want to keep doing this.

On screen, an action sequence heats up, and he leans back to watch. When it's over, he kisses me again.

The pattern repeats whenever a chase or a fight ends. The blanket's almost too warm now, but I feel safer under it. I start sitting up to meet him halfway. Then I wind my arms around his neck. He urges me closer by bracing his forearm around my lower back. I'm folded nearly in half, and it's an odd angle, but I like it. We're perpendicular so this can't go too far.

Besides, Scrap isn't pushing too much. I'm the one getting antsy for the slow parts. My whole body feels more and more hot and achy while Scrap seems content to do nothing but nip at my bottom lip and slide his tongue along mine.

Around three in the morning, Grinder comes home. Frances rouses at the sound of his engine and trots to the door, barking until Grinder stumbles in and gives him one of the treats he keeps on him at all times. It's real sweet until you have to clean wet treat out of the washing machine because some old, drunk biker didn't go through his pockets.

Of course, the kissing stops. Grinder bumps fists with Scrap, scarfs up the half-eaten moon pie and sinks into his easy chair to finish watching *The Expendables* with us.

At some point, I drift off to Scrap and Grinder talking about whether Bruce Willis or Sylvester Stallone kicked more ass back in the day. I'm asleep, but it's a light sleep, and it registers when Grinder shambles off for his bed, and sometime later, when Frances starts whining.

Scrap moves my legs to get up. "Hey, there. Let's let our girl sleep."

A door opens, and I hear the pad of two and four feet head down the stairs. Much later, when I finally wake up fully, Frances is curled up under the coffee table. Sunlight is streaming through the windows, and I'm alone on the sofa. I guess Scrap left. My heart sort of sinks.

I swing myself upright, and I breathe through a wave of dizziness. I drank more than usual last night, and I forgot my meds before I fell asleep. Also, I can feel a freak out bubbling beneath the surface, probably waiting for me to have my coffee to kick in. I can't believe all that happened.

I went out last night. Dancing. And then Scrap Allenbach came home with me, and we watched movies like we were a couple or something, and he took my shoes off and touched my leg. And we kissed. He kissed me, and I kissed him back, and I put my tongue in his mouth and squirmed all up on him, and it was okay. Better than okay.

It was *nice*.

And then there's a noise from the kitchen, and it's not a Grinder noise. I spring to my feet and reach for my knife, but it's on my night stand, and I'm in the living room, and I should run, but Frances is sleeping under the coffee table, and if I bend over to get him, I'll be vulnerable, I *can't* bend over, and I can't leave him, and—

Scrap emerges from the kitchen, shirtless, and leans in the doorway.

"Good. You're up. Where are the coffee filters?"

Up? My heart is in my throat, and I'm on the verge of a

panic attack, about to throw a sixty-pound hound dog over my shoulder and flee.

Oh, God. And my hair is a mess. My jeans have worked themselves around almost backwards. The ass is drooping and the front is wedged up my crotch.

"What are you still doing here?"

"Tryin' to make coffee at the moment." He raises my can of Folgers.

He's not wearing a shirt. His pants hang low, and I can see how his muscles point in a V and a light trail of hair disappears into his—

"Filters?" He's smirking. He saw where I was looking. I am going to die now.

"In the cabinet over the toaster." I flop down onto the sofa and pull the blanket back on top of me. Frances snores.

Why is Scrap still here?

The clock reads ten in the morning. I slept in. I never sleep this late.

There are sounds coming from the kitchen, drawers opening. Is he making breakfast? Unless he wants cereal, he's out of luck.

I stay glued to the couch for a long time before curiosity drives me to see what he's doing. Eventually, I creep down the hall and peek in, trying to smooth my hair as I go.

He's got a carton of eggs and what's left of a gallon of milk on the counter. When he sees me, he lifts up the milk.

"This expired last week."

He holds up the eggs. "These expired last month."

"Expiration dates are more of a suggestion. I read an exposé about them online."

He raises an eyebrow. His bare chest is really distracting. When he turns to dump the milk in the sink, I catch sight of his back. Holy shit. That's distracting, too. All sorts of muscles pop up when he twists at the waist to grab the eggs.

I force myself to look away, and I go pull a box of Cheerios out of a cabinet. "You want some?"

"Dry? No, thanks."

I pour myself a bowl and start eating. It's easier than coming up with something to say.

Scrap turns his attention to brewing the coffee.

"We need to go grocery shopping."

We do? I so don't understand what's happening here.

"Deb buys my groceries when she goes to the bulk store up near Pyle."

"She not been in a while?"

I shrug. She texts me to ask what I need before she goes. Sometimes I'm too in my head to text back in time.

"After we get a shower, we'll go to Save Right. I want to get steaks. You got a grill out back?"

I— Uh. *We* get a shower?

"Yeah. Mom and Dad have one. Um. Scrap? Um—"

Scrap ignores me, pouring two cups, and then takes a stool, sliding a mug to me. He takes a sip and groans, and the sound somehow gets past my nerves and confusion and swirls up the bubbles in my belly.

"That's good."

"It's Folgers."

"It's fuckin' heaven. Now what were you sayin'?"

I can't find my words any better now, so after a moment or two of my stuttering, Scrap says, "You wanna talk about us? What's goin' on?"

"Um. I guess so?" It's not like I want to talk about where this is going or something. It's not like that. I want to know why he's still in my house.

He sets down his cup, draws in a deep breath, and meets my eye.

"I been without you for ten years and nearly a month now. I ain't gonna be without you no longer. You don't want that, tell me now. I'll go. I'll stay gone. But I ain't pussy footin' around you no more like everyone else. You ain't china. You ain't gonna break."

His blue eyes are glued to mine.

"So do you want me to go, or do you wanna get cleaned up and go to the store. Get some filets. Maybe some watermelon and corn on the cob?"

His voice is even, but his body is bracing for impact, his arms set on the edge of the breakfast bar.

I don't have to think as long as I would have thought. "I want watermelon and corn on the cob."

His shoulders relax, and both corners of his lips quirk up.

"I know this ain't gonna be easy or quick. I want you to know I'm a patient man."

"I just don't understand. Why? Why me?"

He seems to think a minute. Then he takes my hand, very slowly, and he lowers it below the countertop to his lap. He presses it to the zipper of his jeans. It takes me a second, but then I realize what I'm touching. He's hard. Really hard, and really big.

Adrenaline surges through my body. If he moved at all, even another inch, I'd probably run. But he's as still as a statue, intently watching my face.

"Every part of me wants you. Always has. I want to hear you laugh, and I want to smell strawberries on your skin, and listen to you, whatever you're talkin' about, don't matter. I don't know why, but I do know it ain't gonna change or go away. I wouldn't want it to."

His dick jerks against my palm. His abs flex tight.

"I want you, Crista. You can't even imagine how bad."

I keep my eyes locked on his, and for once, I catch a glimpse past my own bullshit. It's there, the way he feels, blazing for anyone to see. It stokes a yearning in me, makes me shift on my stool.

"I don't know if I can," I whisper.

"Do you want to?"

"I don't want to try and freak out and ruin everything."

He smiles, and I don't understand why. "You said ruin everything. That means there's something."

I did. I did say that.

"There is something, isn't there." He lifts my hand from his lap and brushes a kiss across my knuckles.

"Yeah, there's something."

"Then let's go grocery shopping and worry about the rest later, when we ain't hungry."

9

SCRAP

Fortune favors the bold. That's what Heavy used to say when we was kids, and he was tryin' to get us to do something that seemed likely to get us hurt, beat by our folks, or arrested. We never did come to ill when Heavy made the plans, but still. He had some crazy ideas back in the day.

Fortune favors the bold.

I honestly don't know what was goin' through my head when I threw Crista Holt over my shoulder like a sack of potatoes. Now, watching her pick through the cantaloupes at the Save Right, I don't really care.

I'm just happy I done what I did.

She's fussin' with the melons, pickin' one up and puttin' it in the cart only to find another she likes better and swappin' 'em out. She's been at it for five minutes now, at least.

I could watch her thump melons forever. Her hair's still damp from her shower, and she's in a new set of ratty hoodies and jeans. No makeup.

She's so fuckin' pretty. She's got this straight little nose and tiny freckles across her cheeks. And her body. I know what's under the baggy men's clothes now. Her skin is soft, and her tits are lush as fuck.

On the sofa last night, when she started getting comfortable, she reached for me, put her arms around my neck, and it was all I could do not to put her on her back and grind into all that soft sweetness. She had those titties squished against my chest, and I could feel her nipples bead through my shirt and hers.

Her eyes got all hazy, and she was risin' up to meet me, pressing a little closer each time I kissed her, smilin' a little more. I was so hard for so fuckin' long my zipper made an impression all the way down my dick.

And I knew, if I pushed too much, she'd go back into her head, start worryin' at shit. So I put myself on a schedule. I let myself kiss her whenever people on the movie was talkin'. They were action movies, so it wasn't that much of the time.

Honestly, I wouldn't have thought I could let myself touch her like I did and hold back. I figured ten years with only my hand, and a few years before that as well, I'd be coming in my jeans as soon as she let me slip my tongue in her hot mouth.

I didn't count on the fact that this is Crista Holt, and she's always made me stronger than I thought I could be. All those years in lock up, so many times I wanted to lay on my bunk and sleep the time away, I made myself get up, work out, read, all because when I got out and saw Crista Holt, I didn't want her to be ashamed of what I was.

So, yeah, I had no problem keepin' my hands from slippin' down those jeans to explore the wetness between her thighs. For that girl, I can do anything.

I know she was wet, too. Before Grinder came home— and I'm gonna have to have a conversation with that motherfucker about movin' out of my woman's place—I could smell her pussy cream whenever she lifted the blanket to get up.

Shit. I move away from the cart to stand over the berry display, like I'm deeply interested in which identical carton I should pick. I better keep my mind off last night, or I'm gonna be starin' at fruit for an hour until my dick calms down.

"You want to get strawberries?" Crista smiles at me from by the oranges, all innocent. That hardness she has at the club is wearin' off, and I can see glimpses now and then of the shy girl I knew before.

"Yeah, baby. Gimme a minute."

Guess spending a lot of time on this shit seems reasonable to her 'cause she just kind of hums and moves on to the vegetables.

"Do you like asparagus?"

I don't know. My dad didn't make it, and they didn't serve it upstate. "Sure."

"I'm going to make you dinner. Steak and asparagus and mashed potatoes."

"You're gonna make me dinner?" I have myself under control so I push the cart to follow her.

"I can cook, you know."

"I believe you."

"I don't very often 'cause—" She kind of trails off. That's her gettin' in her head again. It's so obvious. She slows down and those fingers start worrying the cuff of her hoodie.

"You gonna make me dessert, too, right baby? I want dessert. Chocolate cake."

She shakes whatever it was off, scrunching her nose and smiling again. "I think I can manage that. Did you like the cake Harper got you for your homecoming party?"

"I didn't have any."

"No?" She's throwin' all kinds of things in the cart. Onions. Other onions with stalks. Small onions in bags.

"I was busy tryin' to talk to a girl."

"Yeah?" She's not meetin' my eyes on purpose now. "What did you want to talk to her about?"

"Oh, any old thing. Mostly I wanted to hear about her. What music she likes now. Does she still play the clarinet. Does she think about me."

Crista walks slowly toward the meat section. She's got her hands yanked up in her sleeves. "I don't play the clarinet." Her voice lowers. "But I do think about you. I did."

"What did you think about?" I fall into step beside her and lower my voice, too. There's not a lot of people here so early, and we have the aisle to ourselves, but the whispering seems to turn her cheeks pink.

She nibbles on her bottom lip and my cock jerks. "Riding on your bike. The time you kissed me."

"I thought about you, too."

"You did?" She tilts her head.

"All the time. I'd imagine us, like this."

"In the produce section?"

"Yeah, smartass. In the produce section. And watching TV. And you makin' me dinner."

"And a chocolate cake for dessert."

"And a chocolate cake." I glance over. She seems okay. Her hands have crept out of her sleeves. "I'd think about you at night, too."

She blinks.

"I'd imagine us having a picnic somewhere. Maybe up by Lake Patonquin where we used to have those club cookouts on the beach. We'd be layin' on a blanket, all alone. I'd kiss you, work your dress over your head. Kiss your tits, work my way down to your belly. Settle in between your legs."

"*Scrap.*" She kind of pants my name. Her face is so bright red, it matches the tomato sauce jars.

"I'd taste you. You'd wiggle and squirm, and I'd tongue you 'til you came all over my face."

"*Scrap.*" She tries to hustle and leave me behind, but my legs are long.

"We could do that. Not outside, but in your bed. I could kiss you, just like I did last night. I'll unzip that hoodie and kiss your tits. Then, I'll get you to help me pull down your jeans, and you'll scoot to the end of the bed. I'll kneel on the floor, and you'll put your feet on the edge. And then I'll lick you while I work my dick in my hand."

I'm a little worried that my girl's gonna pass out. I ain't never seen a person's face go so red. She must realize 'cause she pulls up her hood.

"We could do that. No surprises. It would be over the minute you say. I'd stop whenever you want."

I can tell when she understands that I'm serious; I'm not just talkin'. I can see her mull it over in that twisty little brain of hers.

We walk the next few aisles in silence, both of us throwing stuff into the cart.

I've just thrown a box of macaroni and cheese into the cart when she says, "Would I keep my tank top on?"

Holy shit. She ain't sayin' no.

"Baby, you can do whatever you want. You call the plays. Whatever you say goes."

"What if I wanted to do it exactly like that? Would you remember?"

Like I could ever forget. "Yeah. I'd remember."

"And you wouldn't do anything different?"

"I wouldn't change anything up on you. You'd be the boss. You wanna wear a tank top, you wear a tank top."

"It's just—" She glares without focusing down the aisle. "The scars are really bad. Especially the main one."

"It ain't gonna bother me, baby. You don't have to hide shit on my account."

It doesn't occur to me right away that that's a lie, but as we work our way past the boxes of spaghetti, I realize it is. She got mauled. Gutted. When we found her, I used my body to try to staunch the blood—my hands weren't enough. There were flaps of her chest hanging open. The scar has got to be horrible.

That sick rage that used to ride me hard at the beginning of my stint inside rises in my chest like some rotting ghost. I bear down on it, hard.

Crista needs me not to react. It's a tall order, but this ain't about me.

Still, it's hard to drive it back. It takes a minute.

I think she's reading my mind 'cause she starts to talk.

"If we—if we ever did what you're talking about, even if I wear a shirt, you're gonna see some of it. The main scar. It —" She's struggling to get this out, and she's got her gaze glued on the banana display. I don't say anything; I'm so afraid she'll lose her courage. "It starts at the top of my, um, vagina or whatever, and goes all the way above my left boob. Then there's some other smaller scars from the surgeries. Those are more straight and even. Then there are a few other scars from the stabbing. It's kind of a mess."

She stares down at the linoleum. I don't know the right thing to say, and I also know I have to say the absolutely right thing now, and I ain't likely to get another chance if I fuck it up.

I draw in a deep breath. "I know what I'm askin' for."

She glances up. Her brown eyes are hooded and so wary.

"I'm askin' you to trust me, and I understand that ain't a small thing. Maybe I didn't fully get it when I first got back. I get it now."

"I'm really scared." She keeps starin' down those bananas when she says it.

"I know. I'm so fuckin' proud of you."

"'Cause maybe one day I'll get up the courage to let you eat me out?"

I hate the bitterness in her voice, but still, my cock and my heart leap like crazy when she says it.

"Yes, baby. Exactly." And then I laugh and kiss her and hold her hand, and I tease her when she slides a store-bought chocolate sheet cake into the cart.

I need to not fuck this up, and I ain't ate pussy since I was eighteen years old.

CRISTA'S BEEN HOLED up in her room with her sister for two hours. I'm startin' to get nervous. We're goin' to the club-house together tonight. There's a party for Creech's birthday. It didn't occur to me 'til I'd been sittin' here long enough to watch three episodes of House Flippers, but we ain't gone somewhere together before. Not with the MC. We've been keepin' things between just us.

I been stayin' with Crista for a few weeks now. After that first night, I kept comin' back, after my work or hers. She'd feed me more often than not, and she ain't told me to go, so I guess we're shacked up, more or less.

Those first few nights I'd pass out on the sofa with her, but one night, I got a bad spasm in my back, so I hauled her ass to bed. She only grumbled some and went right back to sleep once I tucked her in, and in the morning, I'd left for the garage before she had the chance to wake up and freak herself out about it. That night, we went straight to bed, no fuss. She wears sweatpants, white socks, and a baggy T-shirt to sleep, and I keep my boxers on so she don't get hinky.

There ain't nothing I like better than watching late night TV under the covers with Crista Holt in a fat dude's gym clothes. She wriggles up close to me and nuzzles her nose in my chest. I let my hands wander and stroke the silk where her shirt creeps up. Then we get to kissin', and I'll let my fingers slip under the elastic waistband of her sweats, and sometimes she shies away, but sometimes she throws a leg over my thigh, and I cup her ass, and her eyes go bleary and soft.

I ain't never tamed an animal before, but I'm guessin' it's much like this. No sudden movements. The patience of Job.

I jerk it three, four times a day, and still, I'm hard as a rock as soon as she comes out of the bathroom in forest green sweats and a 2X Van Halen T-shirt with holes in the hem. She must get this shit from Grinder, which is not a thought I like to entertain for long.

Anyway, I ain't pushed for anything, and maybe I'm doin' something right, cause when I mentioned us going out for this birthday shindig, she agreed right off. I realize tonight ain't her usual scene. It's an all call, not only Steel Bones and the usual hang arounds, but Smoke and Steel from up in Shady Gap and a ton of randoms. Creech gets around.

Crista didn't seem freaked out, though. She's been keepin' her hands out of her hoodie and leaving her nails alone. Then Annie showed up, and they disappeared into the bedroom. Even Frances is gettin' nervous. He's dragged his ass down the hallway to whine at her door twice.

I'm about to go get her when finally, the door opens, and—

Damn.

I'm on my feet in an instant.

Annie's leading my girl out, and they're giggling, bringing the smell of strawberry soap and tequila with them. Guess Crista's been nippin' at the liquid courage.

And she's wearin' a dress. Thin straps, the neck cut low, her tits are squeezed up by one of them fancy bras. They're so perfect and creamy like milk.

"You like it?" She's lookin' up from under her eyes, shy and sweet. Annie's done her makeup and put her hair back in barrettes.

"Twirl," Annie orders, and damn if Crista don't, swirling that skirt up past her knees. Her legs are bare, and she's wearin' sandals like she used to, her toes painted pink.

"You're pretty as a picture."

All that skin, her arms, her shoulders, her back. The dress has little birds or some shit on it, and it ain't tight by no means, but it's the sexiest thing I ever saw. I can't help but touch. I gather her up, and she squeals, and Annie laughs. I want to walk her right back into that bedroom, kiss her stupid, but I guess I understand this ain't entirely for my benefit.

"You ready to show off?"

"I'm not showing off." She blushes a soft pink that matches her toes.

"Well, I'm gonna show you off. And you ain't leavin' my side tonight. Understood?"

I see Annie stiffen. She probably thinks I'm gonna trigger our girl. I notice that's how her family handles her. They act like everything's fine, and they ignore her nerves or whatever you want to call it until she's in full freak out. I don't wait. I tell her she's safe all the time.

I see her hands creepin' into her hoodie, I tell her. *I got you.* She starts pickin' at her nails, I tell her. *Ain't no one here but us. Come over and sit beside me.* At first, she'd get embarrassed and fuss. *I don't need you to humor me. I can handle it.*

I kept at it, though, and now she'll sass or huff on principle, and then curl up against me, all shy smiles and soft curves.

Like now. Crista rises to her tiptoes and kisses me, and I curl an arm around her back, tug her closer, push her a step further. My cock goes full mast when I hear the little intake of breath.

Annie clears her throat. "Can you drive? Mom dropped me here on the way to take the kids to Aunt Shirl's."

Guess we're takin' the cage. When I took a gander at what was sittin' in my bank account, Big George showed me some sites on the Internet, and I bought myself a sweet '69 Camaro in Rally Red. Bucket seats, a Muncie 4 speed under the hood, black Z stripes, the whole nine.

"Ladies?" I offer an elbow to them both, and we head off, a little unsteady it turns out. Annie definitely has more than a few under her belt.

It's all fine—great, even—until we get to the clubhouse. Even from outside, I can feel the mood is off. Creech has a lot of associates from when he worked as a tattoo artist, and he's got a lot of other contacts from shadier work he's done in the past. His people are out in force, high strung and loud-mouthed. Their women are worse, sloppy drunk and showin' out. Our sweetbutts are huddled by the pool tables. It's sayin' something when Jo-Beth and Danielle are lookin' down their noses at the guests.

"Is she—? Is that—?" Annie's staring at a naked chick on

a table, covered neck to ankles in tattoos, three dudes lined up while a bare ass pumps away between her legs.

I steer Crista toward the back. Thank God she's checkin' out who's workin' the bar. I know she must've seen worse over the years, but she don't know these people. And I don't need strung-out trash from Pyle fuckin' up my progress.

"Let's go sit by the fire."

It takes Crista a minute to answer. She seems distracted by all the crazy. Steel Bones can rage, but since I been back, we haven't had a crowd this thick, and this off the chain. At least not this early in the evening.

"Crista?"

She shakes herself. "Huh? Yeah. How about Aunt Shirl's spot?"

There's a tree in the way back where Shirl and Twitch used to sit. Twitch would run anyone off who tried to hang there. Kick your ass, too, if you gave him lip about it. He passed from a heart attack when I was inside. He was a great man. Helped me finish restoring my Chevelle.

We get as far as the big bonfire in the yard.

"Scrap!" Creech hollers from where he's sparring with some dude with lobe plugs shaped like helo wheels. "Get your ass over here and wish me happy birthday!"

An unease rises in my gut. A quick scan of the yard shows very few brothers. Cue. Gus. A few of the old heads enjoying the view as some bitches dance topless in front of the makeshift stage. There's no band, but there's death metal blaring from the sound system.

I grab Crista's hand and head over to the bonfire.

"I'm gonna go find Bullet. You give the birthday boy a kiss for me." Annie bails, beating feet back towards the clubhouse.

I glance down at Crista. She still has that deer in headlights look. Her hand is cold and clammy. I'm gonna make this quick.

"Brother." I slap Creech on the back.

"Where's your beer? You didn't get him a beer?" Creech directs this at Crista. My blood rises. He's spittin' whiskey when he talks, three sheets to the wind.

"Just got here, man." I tug my hand back, pullin' Crista a half step half behind me.

"You conceding or what, asshole?" The dude with the gauges stumbles over and throws his arm around Creech's shoulder. He's a piece of work. Septum ring, bridge, nose bone. I do not like the way the fucker is looking at Crista. I could rip his nose off his face. With all the hardware it'd be like opening a Coke can.

Two other dudes with decorator faces wander over. Must be gauges' friends.

"I ain't conceding. Never quit. Never surrender!" Creech lets loose a rebel yell, and the other dudes take up the roar, sending it echoing around the yard. Crista inches closer to me. Yeah. We're done here.

"Happy birthday, man. We're gonna go back in."

"You can't go back. You just got here. You're never around. Saw you more when you were upstate."

"I been busy, brother." I want to turn and check on Crista, but I don't need any attention on her if she's losin' her shit. "Some time this week, we'll go for a ride."

It's like he don't hear me. He's swayin' on his feet, and he lurches closer. The guy with the gauges is nearly holdin' him up now.

"Bullshit. You know you'll be hidin' from that gash or up her ass. You just got out of jail, man. Why you in such a hurry to get locked down again?"

My fist is flying before he finishes, my knuckles cracking

against his cheekbone, snapping his head back. I intend my second punch to lay him flat, but he's already out and crumpling to the ground, and instead, I connect with the other dude with the piercings.

"Motherfucker!"

I open my mouth to apologize, but then there's a soft cry from behind me. Crista. As I turn, the dude comes at me like a hurricane, raining blows at my head, and I drop back, get my arms up, and then there's a scream and a flurry and oh, fuck.

Crista blows past me, dress swishing, and she's screaming, an unearthly shriek, no words, and she's on the guy, slams into him so hard he topples back, and she's got her fists in his hair, and she's just driving his head into the ground over and over again. He's tryin' to buck her off, but her knee's pinning one of his arms, and Gus—God bless fucking Gus—he's dived in and gotten the guy's other arm.

It's a split second before Cue's on him, too, and now he ain't goin' nowhere. Crista's switchin' things up, beatin' the guy however she can, and now she's makin' some sense, screamin' over and over, "You leave him *alone*. You don't *touch* him. I'm gonna fucking *kill* you."

Cue and Gus are cracking up.

"You gonna get your old lady, or we gonna do this all night?" Cue barks at me, smirking while he holds the dude's legs.

"Ow!" Gus yelps. One of Crista's blows went wide. "What I do to you? Scrap, control your woman!"

The crowd's gettin' thicker, and I can see more brothers now. Charge. Wall. Bullet with Annie.

"She's gonna break her hand," Charge says low in my ear, and that sets me moving.

I lift her off the guy, and immediately, she goes limp, all

except her chest, which is rising and falling as if she's run a marathon. I cradle her in my arms, and Wall clears a path for me to carry her back inside. Her face is buried in my cut, and now her shoulders are shaking.

"You don't gotta cry, baby. You won that one." I can't stop the chuckle, not even when she lifts her face to me, wild-eyed and lost, tears streaking down her cheeks. A knot I didn't even know I was carryin' loosens in my chest. My girl can fight.

"I—It's n—not *funny!*"

"Okay." I haul her through the crowd, up the stairs to the bunk I'd been crashin' in before I invited myself into her place. Some of my books are still on the dresser. Looks like no one else has squatted here since I been gone.

I lower myself onto the twin bed, my back against the wall, and I keep her in my lap, arms tight around her. She's starts wrigglin' real quick.

"Let me up."

I raise my hands. She comes up to her knees, straddling me. I'm instantly hard. I keep my eyes up, hope she don't notice. I'm not sure what this mood is. I ain't seen it before. She ain't havin' one of those flashbacks. It ain't a panic attack. Her walls ain't up, either.

She plops her ass down so she's sittin' on my thighs and sniffles.

"That was so fucking embarrassing."

"No, baby. That was sweet as shit."

She wrinkles her nose.

"You were defending me. I was honored."

She slaps my chest. "Quit being an asshole."

"No. I mean it. You took that guy out."

"It was a sneak attack."

"You can sneak attack me, anytime." I'm smilin', and we're jokin', until we aren't.

"I don't want to be the one always losing it." She's worryin' her bottom lip with her teeth. I reach up, smoothing my thumb across that lip.

"Nobody says nothin' when Nickel loses it and beats the shit out of someone." Make bets, yes. Raise an eyebrow? Never.

"Pardon me if I want to be a little less crazy than Nickel Kobald."

"You ain't crazy, baby." She ain't. She's sturdy as shit, my girl. Pulls herself up every time, and pulls herself back from the edge more than I think anyone realizes.

"Why are you always so patient with me?" She curls her fists into my cut. "You know you aren't stuck with me. It's not like once you do time for someone, they own you or something."

"I didn't do time for you. I did time 'cause of what I did." She shrugs like there's no difference. There is, but that's a conversation for a different time. "And that's a stupid fuckin' question."

"It's a serious question."

I think a second. She's sinkin' deeper into her head while I watch, and that ain't a good place for her. "It's like askin' that lady on TV. The one with the white hair and the dragon eggs. It's like askin' her 'how come you're so patient, carryin' around those dragon eggs.' They're fuckin' *dragon eggs*."

"Did you just compare me to Khaleesi?"

I smile and tug her closer. Despite all the talkin', I ain't gotten soft. She's got to feel it. With her wearin' a dress, there's nothin' between us but my denim and her panties. I stroke her thighs, pushin' up the skirt bit by bit.

"Maybe."

"You're ridiculous." Her breath's comin' softer, faster. I take a sip of her lips, smooth my palm up her back. I don't do nothin' I ain't been doin', but maybe it's the adrenaline, or maybe I did somethin' right in a former life, 'cause Crista Holt starts rocking on my dick.

She winds her arms around my neck, and she opens her mouth, lets me slide in. Her cheeks are so red, the heat burns my fingers when I stroke her face and cup her neck. I dare to thrust, not too hard, and I can hardly stifle the groan when she grinds down to meet me. She's all wiggly now, her tits smashed against me, and I hold her tight so she don't come back to earth while I shrug out of my cut and peel off the T-shirt I got on underneath.

I'm keepin' up a rhythm, and thank the Lord the jeans are thick or I'd be coming in my pants. I cup her breast, brush the nipple through the cotton, and she whimpers. She opens her eyes, and they're dopey and so damn pretty.

"Baby," I moan, and she arches her back, ridin' me steady.

"I can keep my clothes on."

What? Her voice is breathy, and big eyes have something else in them now, something sharp. Aware.

"When we talked about this. You said I could keep my clothes on."

Oh, shit. Is this happening? My cock tries to punch its way past my zipper, and my whole body tenses. A wave of hunger crashes through me, like it's been waiting for her words.

"Of course. You're the boss." I take her mouth, and cradle her head in my hands, tryin' to tell her all the things I don't have words for.

"Will you—?" She plucks at my belt, and she eases up

onto her knees a few inches. Oh, fuck. We're doin' that. Yes. Shit. I scrabble at my belt, get it off, unzip my pants, and my cock springs free, red and throbbing.

I ain't a small man, and I brace, watch her face. She's backed up a bit to perch right above my knees. She's eyein' me.

"Baby, we don't have to—" She shuts me up with a finger on my lip.

"Don't say anything. Just...just let me." She reaches out, sort of pets me, and my cock leaps at her touch. She snatches her hand back, and then she giggles, nervous, and reaches out again. She wraps her palm around me this time, and it feels so fucking good. I've got my hands dug into the sheets so I don't do something stupid like roll her over and drive into her. I haven't even touched her pussy. This is some more exploring. We're goin' slow. I knew this was how it'd have to be. I'm good.

And then she reaches under her dress and tugs off her panties. They're white and cotton, and from what I know of women, not the kind they wear when they was plannin' to fuck.

My chest gets tight. I'm fuckin' terrified. Crista crawls back closer to me on her knees. She settles over my cock, and oh fucking Lord, I can feel her hot pussy against the tip of my cock. It's all I can do not to strain for her. She settles her skirt over us so I can't see, and she's got her eyes closed. She's biting that bottom lip again.

"We don't have to do this if you ain't ready, baby."

She shushes me. And then she wraps her fingers around my cock again, and sort of readjusts herself until I'm between her lips. She's soft—so fuckin' silky soft—and hot, but she ain't wet.

She strokes up her pussy with my cock, slow, back and

forth. Her face is all serious concentration. I don't know what to do, and I'm so scared to make the wrong move. My cock ain't got no such compunction, though. It jerks against her, seeking, dripping precum. She uses it to get some lubrication going, and fuck, I'm panting now.

She notches the head of my cock inside her. She's a little wet, but it ain't enough.

"Hold up." I spit in my palm and reach under her dress, try to help, but she's ignoring me, bearing down, and then there's enough slick for me to slip in. Oh, God. It feels so fucking good.

Half of me is watching her face for any sign she's not okay, and the rest of me is so high, in heaven, wrapped in her tight heat as she inches down my cock. She's kneading my shoulders, kind of mumbling to herself, and I can't make out the words, but I know enough not to interrupt.

Her face squinches the deeper I go, and then I'm in to the hilt, and all of nature is urging me to thrust, but I stay still, centered on my woman, and after a long moment, she starts to move.

She buries her face in the crook of my neck, mumbling into my skin, as she works her hips. I don't know what else to do but hold her close, and as the friction steals my sense, pushing me further and further out of my mind, and my cock begins to pulse and balls contract, I start mumbling back.

"I love you, baby. Your pussy is so sweet. I love you. Don't stop. Keep goin'. I love you."

And when I can't take another minute, she sinks down 'til I bottom out, lifting her head and opening her beautiful eyes. My spine tingles, and I shout, cum shooting from my cock, and it's so good, and I know she didn't cum, but her eyes are clear and locked on mine, and it's there, so plain that anyone could see.

Fear.

Fearlessness.

And love.

10

CRISTA

I t's been a week since we did it at the clubhouse.

Every night since, when I come to bed in my sweats, something in Scrap's eyes dies.

He's even more careful with me now. He tries to talk about it. When we're hanging in the backyard, reading. When we take Frances for a walk.

I don't want to talk about it. I never thought I'd do it. Never. Not in a million years. Even now, I can hardly believe I did. But there was something about that night. About kicking that guy's ass. And how fucked up is that?

I don't want to be a head case anymore. I want to be normal. I want to fuck my boyfriend and get off. I want to go to the grocery store by myself to get steaks to surprise him instead of waiting for him to get home from the garage so we can go together.

I'm so done with waiting to be fixed. A little voice whispers to me what needs to be done. What's in the way. I recoil from the thought, shove it deep down.

We're going to do it tonight. Just like we talked about. I'm going to lay on the bed. Take my pants off. Let him see the scars and lick my pussy.

There's a little thrum of excitement in my lower belly, but mostly there's the churn of nausea and panic. It's not just gonna go away. I need to stop being a coward. *Do* something for once.

"Babe? You okay?" Scrap eyes me as he turns off the car.

"Yeah." I hop out and hurry to unload the trunk. I haven't exactly updated Scrap on my plans. I'll be making it clear soon enough, I guess.

After I haul up the first load of groceries, I let Scrap bring up the rest of the bags, and I go hide in the bathroom. Grinder is out—probably at the clubhouse—and Frances is asleep in his bed. It threw me for a minute when I was checking the rooms. The lump in the bed stunk like Grinder, but the foot sticking out of the covers was furry.

In the bathroom, I suck down some deep breaths. I don't have to do this. Scrap will have no problem just grilling steaks. He's so stoked about grilling. It's weird.

Sometimes I forget he's been away for ten years. And then he'll say something like where did the Sears go or what's Alexa. He never talks about his time at Wayne, and I never ask. There's a lot we don't say.

I splash some water on my face and pee. If I'm going to do this, I should take a shower. That requires getting naked, though, and the only way I'm going to be able to do this is if I pretend until the very last possible moment that I am not going to get naked.

Scrap's thumping around in the kitchen, putting stuff away. I brush my teeth. I dribble a little down the front of my hoodie. Crap. The hoodie needs to come off anyway, I guess. I unzip it and hang it from the back of the door. Underneath, I'm wearing a men's ribbed tank top-style undershirt. My white bra-from-a-box shows clearly underneath. It's the kind that has three clasps and no frills. I'm really going to do this wearing this bra?

It's not *like* my mom's bra. It's the same one she wears. She buys them for us both from General Goods.

I undo it and wriggle it off under my tank tops. Now you can see my nipples. That's hot, right?

Oh, shit. Can you see the scars through the material, too?

I tug the curtains open wide for maximum sun and pull the tank taut against my skin. Nips, yes. Scars, no. My panic recedes a few inches. I can do this. He'll see some, but he won't see it all. And I can say stop whenever I want.

If I want to, I can go out to the kitchen right now and say, "Want to watch *London Has Fallen*?" And Scrap will definitely want to watch *London Has Fallen*.

There's a soft knock at the door. I jump in my skin.

"You freakin' out in there?" Scrap's voice is low and amused.

"Yes."

"How come?"

"No reason," I lie. "Like always."

"Cool. I'm gonna go lay down, and play that game Dizzy's kid put on my phone."

"Fortnite?"

"Yeah. That's it."

Okay. He's making this easy for me. He'll be in the bed, and I can saunter in all sexy. It'll go from there.

I put on some deodorant and consider my jeans. They're not boyfriend cut; they're literally a pair of Bullet's old jeans, baggy and faded. They're comfy and...not sexy. They've got to come off. I could drop them, like a strip tease. Scrap would know right away what I'm about.

I should take them off now. The tank top, too. Like ripping off a Band Aid.

Shit. What am I doing? This is not sexy at all. It's one in the afternoon, I'm sober, and this is going to be so awkward.

I sink down on the closed toilet seat.

I need to face facts. There's no way around the awkward. Like Dr. Ang says, recovering from trauma isn't getting back to normal, it's getting used to your new normal.

Working myself up to have sex mid-afternoon with my hot boyfriend while working through the beginnings of a panic attack is my normal.

So what if my normal is weird? Whose isn't?

I slap my knees and stand up, giving my top one last tug down—it's staying on for now—and I head toward the bedroom, checking that the front door is locked and peeking in the closet and pantry and Grinder's room on my way. Frances is still asleep and snoring, tangled in Grinder's sheets.

I open my bedroom door wide, and I don't know what I expected, but it wasn't Scrap, shirtless and lounging on the pillows with my stuffed penguin in his lap, holding up his phone, saying, "Babe! Look at this dude dance!"

I crack up, so I don't notice at first that he's staring.

"Hey," he breathes, and hops up, coming to me, grabbing both my hands and holding them out from my sides. "Look at you." He rakes his gaze down my front, and my nipples pebble even more against my shirt.

I blush; I can feel the heat flood my chest and face, but Scrap's looking down at my legs.

"Yes. Finally." And then he scoops me up, flings me on the bed, lays down beside me, grinning like crazy. "We gonna do this, then?"

"Yeah." Before I can say anything else, his mouth is on

mine, and he's tasting me, tugging and delving deep, babbling when he stops for breath about how long it's been and how soft I am. His hands are ranging everywhere: my thighs, my arms, cupping my cheek.

My mind grows muzzy and slow. Scrap's leaning over me, but his body is next to mine, and it's okay. More than okay. The longer we kiss, the antsier my body gets. I feel the pulsing that I felt back at the clubhouse when he was thrusting up between my legs, and I was so high on adrenaline that the self-consciousness couldn't touch me.

I arch up, wanting to feel the pressure of his bare chest against mine. I let my knees slip apart so he can slip a leg between my thighs. It feels good. More of his body is over me now, but he's moving down, kissing my neck and easing down my tank top, baring my breasts. There are a few white scars noticeable, but they're small, easily ignored.

"Fucking perfect." He takes a nipple into his mouth and sucks, swirling his tongue, and it's almost too much, but it's also not enough. His hands keep roaming, stroking my other breast, then grabbing my hip and urging me up to feel the hardness between his legs.

"Rock, baby," he urges, and I do, and it feels even better. I find a rhythm like the one I set with my hand when I touch myself at night, and he kisses my mouth again, lighter now, softly. He's watching me with his calm blue eyes.

"What?" I pant.

"I'm gonna go down on you now, okay?"

Is it? My skin is hot to the touch, I ache between my legs, and my mind is scattered, but in this moment, it's not from panic, it's from the sensations and the closeness and Scrap, his clean scent and his strong, warm arms. I think it'll be okay.

I nod.

He groans, almost a purr, and he kind of reverses down the bed, tugging me with him. He slips his thumbs in my underwear and pulls them off. I breathe a sigh of relief when he tosses them immediately in the direction of the hamper. If this is my life now, I need to invest in some cute panties.

He does exactly what he said that time at the store, propping my feet on the edge of the bed, then sinking to his knees on the floor. I hear a zipper, and then the heat of his breath on my folds. Oh, God. He's going to see the scar.

Before I can freak, though, he parts me with his fingers and slides his tongue all the way from my clit to my hole, lapping there, moaning words I can't make out because I'm whimpering now, embarrassed, but there's also a tingling in my core, almost an itch, and he stokes it every time he circles his tongue around the swollen bud that's popped out of its hood.

I'm holding onto the sides of my tank top for dear life so it won't inch up any further, but I also can't tear my eyes away from Scrap, his eyes closed as he licks and licks, a blissed out expression on his face when he stops every so often to check on me and give me that half-quirk of a smile.

"Is it good, baby?"

"Yes," I hum, and it is. So good. I'm on my way. Not close yet, but it's building, and that's way more than I thought would happen. I can hear him now, working himself with his free hand, and he's moaning more as he laps up my pussy juices.

This is happening. It's okay, and normal, and I'm normal, and a car pulls into the driveway.

A car door slams. Loud.

Frances barks. Over and over.

There's boots on the stairs. Someone at the door.

I scream.

Footsteps race down the hall.

Oh, Christ.

Oh, Christ.

Gasoline and piss. Cold concrete. Copper.

I kick, draw up my knees and drive my heels into flesh and muscle, over and over—I don't stop; I keep kicking—and there the crunch of bone and screaming, and it's me, and I'm scrabbling for the headboard, and there's blood, spurting, red on the mint green comforter. A man looms above me, and I kick again, digging across the bed with my elbows, reaching for something, anything. A lamp. I pull. It slips from my grasp, falls.

Gasoline and piss. Cold concrete. Copper.

He's still coming, and I tumble to the floor, crawling, fighting to get to the door, digging my nails into the carpet and dragging myself with all I have, and there's a bang—a door—and more footsteps and shouting and barking.

A man yells, "Stop!"

Frances howls.

And I'm crouched in the hallway, shaking—Where are my pants? My underwear?—and there's blood on my leg, but it's not mine. Everything contracts and then comes into perfect clarity, like the focus on the entire world was readjusted.

A sob is wrenched from deep in my chest.

"Get your fuckin' hands off me!" It's Scrap. Oh, God. I hurt Scrap.

He's in the doorway to the bedroom, eyes boring into me, but something's holding him back. I curl in on myself, turn my head into the wall, like that will make this go away, stop the whomp, whomp sound in my ears and the puke burning up my esophagus.

"Not now, brother. Calm down." That's Grinder. There in my bedroom. He's holding Scrap back.

"Baby. Baby, it's okay. It's okay." There's blood streaming from his nose, down his chest, and he's straining toward me. Grinder's losing his grip.

I scream, but it comes out a strangled moan. And then a door slams and Mom comes running. She squats in front of me, a careful distance away, stroking my arm. Frances is standing beside her, facing Scrap, growling low in his throat.

"It's okay, sweetheart. You're okay. Mama's here."

Scrap shouts, lunging forward. "Let me go."

Grinder hauls him back. "Not now."

"Let go or so help me—"

"You need to clean your face first. She can't see you like this." Someone else crowds into the hall. It's Daddy. Daddy's here.

My face burns, and I try to make myself smaller but I can't, try to hide against a wall, but everyone can see me. It feels like there's a hundred people in this narrow hallway. I'm in nothing but a man's tank top, and there's blood splatter on my leg, and I can't breathe. How did I get here?

"Mama, please." I need to turn the volume down. I need to breathe.

"It's all right, sweetheart. Just come with me. I'll take you home. It'll be okay." Somewhere, she's gotten a pair of sweatpants, and draws me to my feet, helping me into them, one leg at a time, and then she walks me out the door and down the stairs, pressing close behind me, sheltering me from everyone's eyes.

I go because I don't know what else to do. Frances pads along behind. There are loud voices behind us, but Daddy handles it.

Mama takes me to her place, and guides me to the bathroom to clean me up. She still has the huge case of bandages and creams from my surgeries, although the packaging is all yellowed a bit from age.

I sit on the toilet seat, sink into the baby blue, plush cover, and let the shaking take over my body while she carefully wipes the drying blood from my leg with a cotton ball soaked in alcohol. I can't tell her it isn't mine. My teeth are clattering too hard.

We don't speak. Frances nudges his way into the room and lays on top of my bare feet. When the shaking starts to subside, Mom pulls me to my feet, and says, "Come on, then. You need a nap."

She's white as a ghost, and her hands are trembling, too. Guilt snakes into my chest.

She takes an orange bottle from the medicine cabinet and gives me two of her little white pills. She grabs me a hoodie I left hanging on the hall tree, and then she walks me to my old bedroom, the one she's redecorated for Annie's kids, and says, "You sleep now. We'll sort it out later."

I sit there like a posed doll.

"Mom. I'm so sorry."

"No need to be."

"I scared you."

"We're fine. We're both fine."

"Did I hurt him bad?" The lump in my throat is so huge I can hardly swallow. "I really hurt him, didn't I?"

"Scrap? He's fine. That's not the first blow to the face that boy took. Not the last either."

She sounds so matter of fact, and if you didn't know Deb Holt, you wouldn't hear it underneath the calm, it'll-be-fine tone of voice. But this is my mother. I can hear the residue of terror underlining her words, just like I can feel it reverberating around my brain as the little pills go to work.

Later, hard to say when since my brain is fuzzy from the meds and the aftereffects of losing my shit, I wake up when the bed dips. I don't even panic. I smell cigarettes and beard wax, and I curl onto my side.

"Daddy?"

"How you doin', little girl?" Pig Iron pats me awkwardly on the shoulder.

"I'll live."

He sighs, looks around the room. It's so incongruous, this pot-bellied biker in stained jeans and a cut, balefully staring at a pink dollhouse and two overflowing hampers filled with stuffies.

"You know, we could put all this shit in the basement. You could move back in."

What? I struggle to disentangle myself from the sheets and sit up.

"Your Ma could use the help when she's watching the girls. I could hang up a flat screen in here. You could watch your shows."

"I'm not moving back in, Dad. I'm twenty-six." My gut swirls with shame and self-disgust. I'm talking like I don't live a few feet away above the garage. Like I'm not buried under the covers in my old bed.

He sniffs like he does when he's aggravated. "My heart cain't take this shit, Crista. I thought you was gettin' murdered."

And now guilt has joined the mix, and I can feel the tears prickling, but there's also something else, the thrum of rage that showed up with Scrap and that seems to dog my steps these days. It's like he showed up, and all the unfairness and the bullshit got thrown into stark relief, and the years of living on edge finally became intolerable. I hate the feeling, but still, I cling to it because however twisted and bitter it is, it doesn't make me weak.

"I'm not moving back in, Daddy. I'm fine."

"Honey, you ain't." He reaches out to smooth my hair, and I duck my head away. I need to get out of here. This room, this place, is backwards. I don't want to go backwards.

I throw my legs over the side of the bed, root around with my feet until I find my shoes.

"Where you goin'?"

"Home." I'm on my feet and woozy, and the idea of walking back to my place, being alone, or worse yet, confronting Scrap, feels heavy enough to almost knock me back into bed. Almost. "I gotta check on Frances."

"Mom'll take care of that."

"Dad. I got to go."

"You got to lay back down. Get some sleep."

I pause by the door. He's still perched on the side of the bed, a sliver of light from the hallway falling across his face. There's gray in his beard, and his forehead's shiny where his hair is receding. His crinkly, brown eyes and his bulbous nose remind me of Santa Claus, just like they did when I was a little girl.

He loves me, and I love him so much. And it's so clear in that moment. Love makes us hostages, me to my secret, to protecting this man who would die for me. And him to his fear, to the memory of cupping my cheek while I bled out on a concrete floor.

We're not gonna be free until we choose to be.

"I'm going home, Daddy. I'll text you when I get there."

"I'll walk you." He goes to stand.

I shake my head. "No, Daddy. It's only next door."

I can't stop him from watching me from the porch, and I can't stop the shuddering as I check the pantry and the closets and under the beds, but I do what I can. Get a shower. Change the sheets.

Hours later, as I'm sitting up straight in bed, alone, my gun resting on the night table, each harmless creak and bark triggering a burst of adrenaline to shoot through my veins, I think hard about choices. And secrets. And what it would take for it to finally, finally be over.

11

SCRAP

G rinder drives me to some dentist's house up in Gracy's Corner. I don't want to go, but he points out that my face makes him want to puke, so how's Crista gonna react?

This dentist is shacked up with a sweetbutt I remember from way back when, a hot blonde named Sunny who used to take on all-comers. He tapes my nose at the breakfast bar in his kitchen, and then he checks my teeth. Crista didn't knock any loose, but she did give me two black eyes. The dentist don't think any other bones in my face are broken. He says I'm lucky.

My girl's got some power in her legs. I need to get back to her, but Grinder makes the point that she always needs a few hours' sleep after a flashback, and my fucked-up face might very well make shit worse instead of better.

So after the dentist, we go to the clubhouse. Pig Iron gets there a little while later. He brings me a beer and nods for me to follow him out to the yard to sit at one of them picnic tables next to the makeshift stage. There's a lot of brothers hangin' out, playing horseshoes. It's a mellow vibe.

I get why I should give Crista space, but I'm startin' to feel antsy. I need to get back to her. She's gonna be hurtin', tellin' herself all kinds of fucked up things. I know we ain't been together long, but I know my girl. If she gets deep in her head, she's gonna make it ten times worse. And it ain't the end of the world. I've accepted that lovin' Crista Holt comes with a shit ton of baggage, and that's fine by me.

Maybe I need to rethink sex positions, but this kind of shit ain't something I can't handle.

I chug my beer, clear that I have other places I want to be. Pig Iron gives me a look when I thump the empty on the table.

"Boy, you ain't goin' nowhere until we've had ourselves a nice, long talk." Pig Iron cracks open another bottle and slides it to me. "Get comfortable."

I grin. "Is this the talk where you tell me you got an unregistered sawed-off under your bed and ain't no one gonna find me if I lay a hand on your little girl? Cause you gave me that talk already about twelve years ago."

"I don't need to warn you off with a shotgun. Looks like my girl can fuck you up just fine with her bare feet."

I snort, and Pig Iron chuckles. We both sober up soon enough.

"Nah. This ain't that." Pig Iron exhales, wipes his beard. "This is where I ask if you know what the fuck you're doing."

"Fuck no, I don't know what I'm doin'. Do you guys?" I keep my gaze steady. He needs to know that I respect him as a brother and as Crista's father, but at the end of the day, she's mine.

Pig Iron shakes his head. "We've always took it day by day. Did whatever the doctors told us to do. Tried to push her, but not too hard. She's gotten better." Pig Iron eyes my face. "You can't push her too hard, too fast. Some shit she just might never be ready for."

We both shift uncomfortably in our seats, take long sips from our beers. This ain't the kind of conversation you want to have with your woman's father.

"Listen," Pig Iron finally says. "The only thing that's ever worked with Crista is let her do shit in her own time. I mean, going back to when she was a baby even. Deb would buy those walkers. She'd try to bribe her with animal crackers and shit. Crista does things in her own time. When she was ready, she walked."

"Yeah?"

"Deb and I were at the bar. We'd left her on a mat by the pool table, and we look up, and there she was, holdin' an eight ball."

"I don't know. My experience is she needs a little push."

Pig Iron's fist clenches. "I know you care. But you gotta understand. She might not be *able* to be with you how you want."

He looks up to the sky like he's wishin' someone would rescue him.

"I get what you're sayin'."

"I love you, brother, but I don't know if you do. The fucker— He stabbed her, and then he raped her, and then when he was done, he slit her open. She can't have kids." Pig Iron's voice is cracking, and puke is burning up my throat. "No offense, but you been back a month or so. Do you really think that's all the time it takes to get over somethin' like that?

Now it's shame roiling my guts. 'Cause put like that? No. I don't think me bein' here a hot minute, puttin' my foot in my mouth more often than not, is enough to overcome somethin' like that.

I pushed, though. I wasn't an asshole about it, but I pushed. And Crista's brave as shit. She's shy, and she ain't like some poster child for survivors, but she ain't a quitter, neither. I pushed, and she let me, and this is what happened. Five steps backward.

"Shit, Pig Iron."

I love this man like a father. I got to respect what he says.Dad passed when I was in high school, about a year before the shit went down with Crista. After losing Mom like we did, and then Dad goin' so sudden, I wasn't doin' so good. Twitch, George, Boots—they all stepped up for me. My dad was Steel Bones, a brother, and that made me their son. With Pig Iron, it always felt like more. Like he saw somethin' in me. If he's tellin' me this now, I got to listen.

If he says I need to give Crista space, it don't matter that my muscles are achin' from the strain of holding myself back. I can bear it.

I'm about to get myself another beer when a shout goes up from inside the clubhouse. Pig Iron and I exchange a look and then we're haulin' ass, along with the other brother who'd been milling around in the yard.

As soon as we're in the main room, I catch the name *Rebel Raiders*.

Heavy's on the phone, and Forty's got the safe open, handing out pieces, barking orders to saddle up.

I lope over, hold out a hand. Forty slaps a Walther in my palm. I check the chamber.

"Bad, eh?"

Forty grunts.

Heavy's been keepin' me so sidelined, I feel like I been up in the stands. This must be some shit if I'm gonna ride. Ain't gonna lie. Feels good.

"Listen up!" Creech hollers, and the dozen or so brothers get instantly silent.

Heavy shuffles forward, Dizzy at his side lookin' like hell. The two could be brothers with their wild, long black hair, even though Dizzy's clearly got some years on Heavy, and Heavy's got a half-foot and sixty pounds on Dizzy.

"Roosevelt, Fay-Lee, and Story are up at Twiggy's by the county line, and they've run into some Raiders. We don't know what this is, but Knocker Johnson made very clear we ain't at peace no more. We go in hot."

Then he hollers like he's herding steers, and the club moves out at a run and mounts up. I take the time to call Crista and leave a message before I turn my engine and fall in line, toward the middle of formation. We haul ass out of town, and even though it's been a decade since I rode on a mission like this, the rhythm is there, part of my muscle memory.

It's late afternoon, the kind of day when the sun shines warm but not hot, and my heart's pumpin' hard in my chest, for once not for some fucked up, heavy reason, but because I'm with my brothers, ridin' like cowboys into some mess I didn't have shit to do with.

A weight lifts off my shoulders. The gun's slick against the small of my back, and I push thoughts of Crista straight out of my mind. She's safe at her mother's. Fixing that shit will save for another day.

I let it go, for the first time, and even though I'm ridin' into the unknown, I feel light as air, free as the wind buffeting my face as my brothers and I race for the county line.

12

CRISTA

There's no cell service at Heavy's cabin. It's hardly in what you'd call the mountains—low rolling hills more like—but it's far enough out in the boondocks that you can't get a signal. Even if I'd wanted to, I couldn't have called Scrap until we were driving home, and I got service back.

It's been two days since the Rebel Raiders attack at Twiggy's, and Heavy's loosened up the lockdown. It was fucked up. The Raiders happened on Fay-Lee, Story, and a prospect at a roadhouse in the middle of nowhere. They almost kidnapped Fay-Lee, and they almost killed the prospect when the club arrived.

I heard about it piecemeal from Annie and a few other old ladies who'd been bunking at Heavy's place. Mom wouldn't tell me shit. She's still treating me with kid gloves, which is fair enough, but she should know by now I bounce back. Not full up, but I don't stay down.

The news is eating at me, though. I spent the whole time at Heavy's cabin fixating on the Rebel Raiders. After Scrap killed Inch Johnson, the Raiders more or less fell apart.

Some of them still hung around up near Shady Gap and Pyle, dealing meth and dwindling down to almost no one as the cops and the opioids whittled away at them. Since I didn't leave town, they weren't in my face except when I drove past the gas station across from Finnegan's Ice Cream.

Then a few months ago, they trashed the Patonquin construction site and then The White Van. My nerves got even janglier than usual, and I started tagging along with my mom to the shooting range again. It didn't seem to turn into anything, though. But now? The Raiders are trying to kidnap an old lady and kill a prospect in broad daylight?

I haven't been able to sleep without popping three of Mom's Xanax, so I'm dopey and jumpy at the same time which is ridiculous. A kid will slam a door, and a minute later, I fall out of my chair.

I want Scrap, but I have no right after how I lost my shit on him, so I take it minute by minute, the way Dr. Ang taught me when I first got out of the hospital. I focus on getting out of bed. Sit up. Throw my legs over the side. Stare until I work up the energy to stand. Then I talk myself through getting showered. Wash my hair. Brush my teeth. Hang the towel over the shower curtain rod. That's how I do my day, coaching myself to put one foot in front of the other, then do the next thing and the next, until it's dark enough that I can go lie in bed and stare at the ceiling.

I try to tell myself that what happened with Fay-Lee has nothing to do with me—the past is the past, this is some new bullshit. But what happened back then? It didn't have anything to do with me either.

So I try so hard to shove it all to the back of my mind, think about *anything* else, so of course, then I think about Scrap, and my entire body burns with the humiliation. I broke his fucking *nose*. The whole thing is all disjointed and hazy, but I remember it wasn't just a single, startled kick. I kept going, stomping. I think he fell. I think he raised his hands to try to protect his face. He has to hate me.

He must know it's not worth it now. I'm not worth it. And goddamn if he couldn't have accepted that weeks ago, before I let him in. Before he kissed me, and we watched movies, and he moved in, and we fucked, and I thought that maybe I could be normal. I could have a normal life.

But I can't be normal, and that's my fault. Just like what happened back then was my fault.

You know, when you try really hard not to think about things? *Everything* comes up. Your baggage comes spewing forth, cackling and chittering like those swarms of locusts you see on those History Channel reenactments of the ten plagues of Egypt.

See, I don't remember much about what happened after the attack. But I remember before in painful, perfect detail.

I had to stay after school, but it wasn't a band practice day. I needed to retake a test in Spanish. I called home after I was done, figuring someone would come get me, and Mom told me she was in Pyle on a shopping trip with Aunt Shirlene. Dad was busy. Mom said hold tight. She'd find someone to get me. She was pissed that I hadn't planned ahead.

I asked why didn't she call Scrap and have him get me?

Mom said Scrap was a grown man, not my personal chauffeur.

And I was pissed. I'd gotten my hopes up. Maybe I'd even planned it so that I could see him. Ride behind him and breathe in the leather of his cut.

I sat on the front steps of the high school, and one-by-one, the other kids who stayed after got picked up. The sun got lower, and it got chilly. I was wearing a yellow sundress with spaghetti straps, and I'd forgotten my hoodie. The one I always wore.

I got bored, and my butt got cold sitting on the concrete. I decided to start walking home. It was only a few miles. Whenever Mom got ahold of someone to get me, she'd call. I'd tell them where I was. At this rate, I'd probably be home before she rounded up anyone to pick me up.

So I started down Main Street toward Gracy Avenue. I passed the post office. Finnegan's Ice Cream. The diner. I was walking along the stretch of Gracy Avenue near the turn off for Route 12 when an old Impala pulled over. The driver waved me over.

He said something over his shoulder to a guy slouched in the back.

"Hey. Can you help me?" he asked.

I'm not stupid.

I knew what men were capable of. I was sixteen, not six. Not that long before, a Rebel Raider had taken a baseball bat to Hobs Ruth's head. And the men at the club, most were like my dad and Bullet, but some were not. Some disappeared all of a sudden, and sometimes, the women who hung around had black eyes.

I was raised around hard, loud, drunk men with tempers and addictions and bad habits. I wasn't stupid.

But a strange man said, "Hey. Can you help me?"

And I walked right over. I didn't stop to think for a single second. I was worried about the Spanish test and Scrap Allenbach and how my feet hurt walking so far in flip flops.

"You're Pig Iron's kid, right?" The man had been smiling. I think I smiled back.

And I said yes. I *heard* the man say, "It's her. Get her."

I heard him, and I didn't move. I stood there, waiting. What the fuck for?

By the time the back door flew open and the other man dragged me in, shoving me down in the foot well, it was too late. It all happened so quickly, but not so quickly that I couldn't have run. Or screamed. Or fought.

You see, it was all on me. Scrap going away? That was on me. Every day since Mom and I pulled into the gas station across from Finnegan's Ice Cream, when I sat frozen in horror while the motherfucker who dragged me into Inch Johnson's back seat pumped our gas and joked with my mother about the Steelers, when he winked at me, no recognition on his face.

Every day since then, I've kept my mouth shut. I am not going to be responsible for another life ruined. My dad or Heavy or another brother in jail or dead, it's *not* going to be on me.

Right now, as I sit tense and nauseous in the car, I listen to the girls chirp happily in the back while Annie sings along to the radio. Destroying this family is *not* going to be on me.

When there's finally service, I see I have a voicemail. With a stone in my gut, I listen to it, and then I beg Annie to pull over the car, and I puke on the side of Highway 11 until I'm dry heaving, gravel digging into my knees.

Hey, baby. I'm fine. Don't worry about my nose. Ain't gonna lie, it's probably an improvement. Listen. There's shit going down, but I don't want you to worry. It's gonna get taken care of. I'll call after it's settled.

You change your mind about—You need me, call me. Anytime. I'll come runnin'.

That was three days ago. There is no other message. No other missed call.

When my stomach's empty, I look up, and Annie's two

oldest have their faces pressed against the backseat window, worry rounding their eyes. Annie's staring at me.

Mom's riding home with Dad. Thank the Lord they're ahead of us, or I'd have an even bigger audience. As it is, Bullet's pulled his Fatboy off on the shoulder a yard behind us. He's escorting us back to town. Dad bet him a hundred bucks that if he tried anything with Annie, Dad would cut off Bullet's dick and sew his patch in its place. Bullet's been keepin' a good, healthy distance this whole drive.

"I'm good. Just carsick." I wave at my nieces and my ex-brother-in-law. The girls blink and cast scared looks at Annie. Oh, God. The shame is bitter in my mouth. I force myself to get back in the car, buckle myself in.

Scrap is fine. If he wasn't, someone would have told me.

Would they, though? Or would they treat me like a breakable nut case the way they always do?

"Annie? Is Scrap okay?"

"Far as I know."

I need to keep it together. Think this through. History is not repeating itself.

There's shit going down, but I don't want you to worry. It's gonna get taken care of.

Scrap went after the Rebel Raiders again, and he's on parole. Best case scenario, he got arrested. He gets sent back to SCI Wayne to serve out his sentence. Worse case scenario? He lost this time, and he's dead, and no one will tell me because they think I'm too weak to handle the truth.

If I hadn't lost my mind, I'd have been with him. If I were there, he wouldn't leave me. He wouldn't do anything stupid.

Oh, yeah? He left you the other day.

Dad told him to back off. I was having a flashback.

Or your shit is too much. Maybe he'd rather risk losing his parole than figure out how to get rid of your crazy ass.

"You okay?" Annie's giving me a hard look.

"Carsick." I dare her to question me. She shrugs.

I need to find Scrap. Talk to him. I think about calling, but I need to see him. I need to let him know that it's okay. I understand if I'm too much. He doesn't need to mess up his life again.

"Can you drop me at the clubhouse?"

Annie raises an eyebrow.

"I want to see Scrap."

"All right, lover girl." Annie makes the turn onto Route 9, and I dig in my purse for a mint. It's an old purse from middle school. Denim with fringe. When we came out to the cabin, I wasn't about to go without my Beretta, so I needed a way to carry it. It was hard enough leaving Frances with the neighbors, although Frances didn't seem bothered. I wasn't leaving my gun.

It only takes twenty minutes or so to get to the clubhouse. Annie asks me if I can get a ride back to Mom and Dad's, and from a yard back, Bullet hollers, "I'll see her home."

Annie pulls out and leaves me alone, surrounded by dozens and dozens of bikes and trucks and SUVs. Everyone and their mother is here. I scan for Scrap's bike, but I don't see it. That doesn't mean anything. The parking has overflowed into the field across the street.

As I walk in, it strikes me how similar the vibe is to the night Scrap came home. The drinking has clearly been going for some time, and there's music and chatter and weed in the air. They've got two prospects—Wash and Boom—tending bar.

I've walked through this old hangar a thousand times,

but today, it feels different. I feel different. Like I've walked off the map, and I'm not sure anymore where I'm heading.

I don't see Scrap until I'm almost to the bar. He's at a table with Harper Ruth. He's smiling, not his usual half-smirk, but a full smile that crinkles the corners of his eyes. Her hand is resting on his forearm. He's not doing a thing about it.

Harper has a glass of wine in front of her like always. She empties it, and then Scrap hands her his beer. She winks as she tips it back.

And then he sees me, and his smile disappears.

Guess I shouldn't have worried. He was just fine. What should have been relief feels like a fist in the mouth.

SCRAP

I've been on my bike the past seventy-two hours, beatin' the bushes for a skinny man with a snake tattoo and a fucked-up eye. Dude is a ghost. It don't help that the Rebel Raiders' known associates tend to be high as shit or baked crispy. They don't make for the most coherent informants.

When Heavy called us in with a lead, I can't say I wasn't grateful. I ain't spent this much time in a saddle since I was twenty, and I guess my ass could take a hell of a lot more then. Besides, Crista will be back in town soon. On the phone, Heavy said he's easing up the lockdown.

When we got to Twiggy's three days past, two Raiders were takin' turns beating Roosevelt to death while a third, the skinny guy, tried to drag Fay-Lee into a car. If not for Story Jenkins....Well, it don't bear thinkin' on. Dizzy's called chaos, and Heavy seconded. The man with the snake tattoo's as good as dead.

When I roll up to the clubhouse, the lots so full, I got to park in the back of the field across the street. Guess some people ain't got the news about the lockdown gettin' lifted.

I need a shower and a decent meal, and I need to talk to Crista. She's fine. Pig Iron and I have been in contact, but still. Sooner's better. She ain't tried to call me as far as I know. The service is bad up at the cabin, but...I don't need to think about that right now.

When I get inside, Forty greets me at the door. Tells me to rest, church is in an hour. We got a heads up on the location of the dude—his name's Donny or Danny—and we've got eyes on him. Apparently, he's a real dumb fuck. He's at work like nothin' happened, a few miles away.

I wash the road off and borrow some threads. I can't wait to get home. Then it strikes me. Do I even have one?

What am I gonna do? Push my way back into Crista's place again? Pretend none of this happened? My nose is still taped, and my eyes got yellow and brown rings around 'em like a fuckin' raccoon.

If she wants this—if she's ready for this—I need to stop pushin'. Leave be.

The thought leaves a taste like dirt in my mouth. I head for the bar, order a beer. They've got the prospects workin' it. The one called Boom's a smartass. A college dropout from up in Pyle. He's still tryin' to grow out his ironical mutton chops.

"What'll you have, my man?"

"Whatever's good."

"All right, all right." He goes into the fridge and passes me some hipster shit. The label's so artsy I can't tell what it's called.

I take it to a table. Don't think my ass could take a bar stool right now. I sip, not expecting anything, but it's real good. Reminds me of the shit Twitch used to brew in his basement.

I ain't thinkin' about much when Harper Ruth slides into

the seat beside me. She's got a glass of red wine, per usual, and she's dressed like she's goin' to court, fancy white blouse and a black skirt.

"Whatcha doin', little brother?" Her wine sloshes a little when she sets it down. Woman's tipsy.

"Waitin' for church."

"You haven't come to see me." She slaps my chest. Drunk Harper's always handsy. "You don't need a lawyer anymore, and I'm yesterday's news?"

"You know you're always my girl."

Harper's face takes on a pinched look. Hurt, almost, which don't make sense. "No one's ever gonna be your girl except Crista Holt. Everybody knows that. Sad as shit, but true nonetheless."

"I didn't think you were holdin' a torch for me, Harper Ruth." This conversation is goin' in a strange direction. Until about a year ago, Harper was Charge's old lady. Then she dropped him for Des Wade, a shady country club type with his hands in most everything around these parts. Word among the brothers was she wanted to climb the ladder a rung or two, see how the other half lives.

"You know I love you, little brother, but not like that. It just kills me to see you fight so hard for a woman who won't fight for herself."

I tense, lean back. That ain't fair.

"If I had a man who loved me like you do Crista Holt, I'd do anything for him. Be anything for him."

"You didn't even let Charge get the kind of dog he wanted." Charge bitched about that a whole visit up in Wayne. He wanted a Great Dane. He got a Corgi. "How is George?"

She drains her wine. "He's good. And Charge didn't love me for shit. He wouldn't have moved on so fast if he did."

"Weren't you fuckin' Des Wade before you and Charge split?"

"Semantics." She waves her hand.

"That ain't what that means."

Harper holds up her finger. Her gaze is unfocused, and she's tilting a little in her seat. Yeah, the woman's feelin' it. "I got my reasons, Scrap. As do we all. Now you gonna pass me that pussy beer you're drinkin', or are you gonna get me another glass of wine?"

"You always been bossy as shit, Harper." I smile, and she rests her hand on my forearm. I pass her the beer.

"You always been too good for this world, little brother. Too good for me, for sure."

It's then I notice Crista Holt in her mint green hoodie, standing twenty feet away. The lightness from all the ridin' disappears, and I'm hit again, like I am every time, with the weight of her. Her skin's sallow, and her hands are tucked up in her sleeves, and every fiber in me wants to go to her, throw her over my shoulder, take her upstairs and kiss every inch of her until I'm certain she's real cause there's no way she can be.

There's no way that a man can walk around with his heart twenty feet across the room. It ain't possible.

I will her to come to me. Just a step. A wave, even, but all she does is stand there, her face frozen, her eyes shuttered.

And I can't take it. I scoot my chair back, and I stand, and when she doesn't make a move, I turn and walk toward the stairs up to the bunks.

And every step I pray she follows, but I know she won't.

That's my heart, standing across the room, stuck in place, and somehow, at the same time, my heart is breaking too, inside my chest.

14

CRISTA

When he's gone, it's like my feet come unglued from the floor. I can hardly breathe. He walked away. He finally walked away.

Like I'm on autopilot, I wander over to where Harper's finishing off the beer he left. When I get close, she sprawls back in her chair, and from how much she flounces when she does it, I know that she's not sober, and she's spoilin' for a fight.

She's been drinking a lot more since she ditched Charge for Des Wade. I guess with more money comes more problems.

"Well, well. Crista Holt. Shouldn't you be in a pretty white dress, tied to a railroad track somewhere?"

Her eyes are shiny, and there's a drop of Merlot on her satiny white blouse. For Harper Ruth, she's a hot mess.

"What the hell are you doing with Scrap?"

"Oh. Now you want to make some kind of claim? I just saw him walk off same as you. I don't think it matters much what him and I are up to."

"Leave him the fuck alone."

"Or what? What are you gonna do? Hide behind the bar? Under a shelf in the storage closet? I know. Above your daddy's garage?"

I grit, ball my fists. This isn't what I need to be doing. I need to go after Scrap. Talk to him. Make all this wrong right somehow. "Fuck off, Harper. Stay away from him."

"Why? What exactly are you gonna do with him, Crista Holt, besides the same thing you bitches always do? Let a man fight your battles? I'm sick of all you weak, little—" Harper plunks her glass on the table. "You know what?"

There's a huge knot in my stomach, and her words twist it tighter.

"In an hour or so, in that room—" She jerks her thumb at the room with the big table, where the brothers hold church. "My brother is gonna decide to kill a man. He's gonna put his life on the line—again—and Scrap's and Charge's and Forty's and all of them because some dumb bitch was stupid and put herself in danger. Again."

My mouth goes dry. What?

"Yeah. They found the Rebel Raider who attacked Fay-Lee. Some creepy fuck with a cloudy, white eye. Dude's like a Bond villain. Tattoo of a snake on his neck. The eye from the old man from 'The Tell-Tale Heart.'"

My blood floods to the floor, and I sway against the table. Oh, God. It can't be. Acid scores my throat. It cannot be.

"Oh, don't get upset." Harper curls her lip. "The men will clean up this mess, too. And if it costs them a few years of their life? Won't be the first time, right?"

"Oh, God." I cover my mouth with my hand.

Harper stands, shaky until she braces herself on the table, too. "Go home, Crista. There's nothing for you to do here. The prospects have the bar covered. And what else can you do, anyway?"

She spins away, and that's fine, because I'm already staggering for the bathroom. I take out my phone. Trace the letter *F*. Pull up the pic. His face pops up, and my stomach heaves.

There he is. Donny Mulvaney. His face is in profile so you can't see the eye with the cataract. The picture is five years old, before he got the color filled in on the snake tattoo. In this pic, it's only an outline.

When I was sixteen, and he took his turn after Inch Johnson on the floor of an abandoned gas station on Route 12, he didn't have any tattoos at all. Just that cloudy eye. Like a white marble.

I slam to my knees, and my phone clatters to the tile floor. The screen cracks. I wretch into the toilet, but nothing comes up.

Oh, God. This is on me.

I thought if I kept my mouth shut, we'd all be safe.

I thought he wasn't in the life anymore. He had a job, he worked the 7 to 3, and he was never late. I never once saw him in a cut or with a bike. I figured he'd gone straight. He'd been out-of-his mind high that day. He never even smoked now. Didn't even chew.

When Mom and I ran into him that day, I'd been a foot away from him, and he'd looked right at me, but with my hair cut and the extra pounds, he had no idea who I was. I didn't have to do anything. I could tuck his existence away in a corner of my mind, tell myself it's the past. I'm safe, and if I keep my mouth shut, no one else would get hurt.

I told myself that, and I didn't look to closely at Donny Mulvaney. Never followed him home. Never looked him up online.

'Cause I knew.

If I told Dad, he'd kill him. If I told Heavy or Grinder or any of the brothers, they'd kill him. And maybe they'd get away with it like with Dutchy. Or maybe it'd all be fine until the Rebel Raiders ran into another girl walking home along Gracy Avenue. Like maybe one of Annie's little girls.

So I watched him. Checked him like the locks and the windows and the empty rooms of my house. And I lied to myself. Told myself that it was over. I could live with what he did to me. What they did to me. I could bear it forever if no one else got hurt.

But it's not over. It'll never be over.

Harper's right. I can't hide anymore.

I haul myself off the bathroom floor, wipe my face with brown paper towels, and go back to the bar.

Scrap gave up ten years for me. So I could do what? Hide behind a bar. Above my father's garage?

Harper's sitting where I left her, leaning precariously over the side of her chair.

"I need to borrow your car."

"The Audi? Hell, no." Harper peers closer at my face. "Are you *crying*, Crista Holt? Damn. Wipe your face."

I touch my face. It's wet. The paper towels just smeared the tears around. Whatever. "Give me the keys, Harper."

"Fuck that. You're gonna have one of those attacks and drive my car off the road."

"I need it." I step toward her, fists clenching.

"Go find Mommy and ask for her keys. Shit. Scrap just went upstairs. Ask him."

"I need to borrow yours."

"Well, unfortunately for you, unlike the entire Holt family and Scrap Allenbach, I don't get off on rescuing your pathetic, fat ass from your own fucking helplessness."

She smiles triumphantly, even raises her glass, and it's like a cork pops. All the anger that's been bubbling up since Scrap came home, all the pent up rage from years of everyone treating me like I'm gonna break when the shit I carry has made me hard as steel, all of it comes flying out, and my fist is driving into her face before she can put her glass back down.

She screams. Her chair falls backwards with her still in it. Her glass goes flying, shattering on the floor, and I'm on her, whaling away, and she's bucking and flailing, trying to dislodge me, but I'm bigger, and I'm fucking done with her mouth.

Vaguely, I register hooting and cheering, and then she gets a chunk of my cheek with her nails, and I double down, lift her up by the hair, and I'm about to slam her head into the floor when a massive arm lifts me off of her.

She scrambles right up, screaming, "You goddamn *ingrate*. You have no idea what we've done for you!"

"What the fuck have *you* ever done for me?" I'm straining against the arms holding me back. It has to be Wall. No one else is this big.

"I— I—" I can tell there's something she wants to say. It's written all over her face. But her eyes dart from me to Wall to all the brothers gathered around to watch the show. Her face shutters, and damn, but I recognize that look. Harper Ruth has secrets of her own.

She sighs, touches her fingers gingerly to her quickly bruising cheek. "You know what? It doesn't matter. The keys are in my purse."

"Thanks." I rummage in her purse while she calls the brothers a bunch of nosy fucks and tells them to fuck off, the show's over.

When I find the keys, I give her a nod, and I bail, jogging

to the car, half afraid someone will stop me, half afraid no one will. My knuckles throb, and my mind is racing. I don't know what I'm going to do, but I can't do nothing. Not anymore.

It takes ten minutes to drive to Finnegan's Ice Cream. There are a few customers, but they're parked close to the building. My usual space is open. Traffic is light on Gracy Avenue at this time of day between lunch and quitting time. Across the street, the garage is open; the bay doors are up.

And there he is. My stomach heaves.

Donny Mulvaney is working the full-service pump, like always. He's wearing a stained white T-shirt and black jeans. His long, greasy hair is tucked behind his ears. He's smiling at the customers, joking with a woman pumping her own gas.

I sit there a long time, watching, working at the holes in the cuff of my hoodie and gnawing at the inside of my cheek, while Donny Mulvaney smiles at customer after customer.

Back when I was sixteen, when he took his turn on the gas station floor, he'd smiled at Inch Johnson the whole time. That same desperate, *please like me* grin.

My entire body shakes harder the longer I stare, my teeth clacking until I grind my jaw shut to put an end to it. If I wait any longer, I'll be frozen in place. I could lose my shit. Any second, I could fly off into the past, my own brain could squeeze the breath from my lungs. I need to move. Do *something*.

I dig in my purse, fumble with the gun, disengage the safety. I slip it into my hoodie pocket.

I'm just going to walk over there. If I'm there, nothing can happen. Nothing worse. It's like in all the horror movies. You look into the monster's eyes, and you take away its power. You force yourself to be brave, and the God in the machine sorts the rest.

I know it's bullshit, and I know that's not how the world works, but still, I force myself to swing open the car door and take a step toward the man who grinned while I pleaded for my life.

I'm whimpering, so I shove my busted up fist in my mouth.

Oh, God. I don't want to do this. I don't want to do this.

Ever since I curled into a ball and begged Inch Johnson not to kill me, told him I'd do anything he wanted, ever since then I've known what I am. A coward. But still, I force one foot in front of the other.

I pull my hood up, and I fight for a deep breath as I walk across the road.

15

SCRAP

I wait a long time in that twin bed where Crista and I fucked. Was that only a week or so ago? I wait and hope, and as the minutes pass, and it gets clearer and clearer that she ain't gonna choose me, I wait and wish that shit was different.

When the knock finally comes on the door, it ain't her. It's Forty.

I sigh and try to shake it off. "It time for church already?"

"Not quite yet. Can I sit?" Forty ducks through the door. I shrug, gesture to a stool.

"We found the guy, eh?" I guess.

Forty lowers himself, back straight as board. Just lookin' at the fucker has always made me uncomfortable. He had a military mien before he ever signed up.

"Yeah. Found out the guy's road name is Rattler. Real name is Danny or Donny. Get this. He works at the gas station on Gracy Avenue."

"No shit."

"Dude is there as we speak, pumpin' gas. We got eyes on him."

"Rebel Raiders weren't never ones for brains, were they?"

"That they weren't. You ask me, though, this guy's only the first in line." Forty's face hardens into a scowl.

"Who's next?" I start to see that this isn't a social call. Forty's politicking before church. He's got a move he wants to make, and he wants to see if I'll back it.

"After this is handled, we need to go after Knocker Johnson hard. He's the reason these pissants are gettin' bold. Before he came back, the Raiders were blowin' themselves up in trailers out in the woods. Now they're tryin' to fuck with our business? Our women?"

"It's the blown job, man. Blowin' up in our faces again," I say. You look back far enough, all the shit that goes down in Petty's Mill can be traced to that one botched job.

"Past ain't the past," Forty agrees. "Not for a man who lost twenty years of his life." He looks to me. I nod.

This is the truth. When I heard that Knocker Johnson was spending his freedom fucking with Steel Bones, I asked Heavy why he didn't take him out. Whatever Knocker once was, he's an enemy now.

Heavy, that mystical motherfucker, just said, *Acquitting the guilty and condemning the innocent—the Lord detests them both.*

It don't make sense to me, but I ain't a club officer, and I never had a desire to be.

"If I call chaos on Knocker at church, can I count on your aye?" I do like how Forty cuts to the chase. I'm about to agree when there's another light knock on my door frame.

A woman's knock.

My heart thuds against my ribs, and I feel instantly lighter. Then Harper Ruth stumbles in. She's in her stockings now, no shoes, and she's swinging a bottle of red by the neck. And somehow in the last few minutes, she earned herself a black eye.

"Can I help you?"

Harper sighs, and she sways on her feet. "You know how I am when I get drunk? How I can be a real cunt?"

Forty snorts.

"Yeah," I say. "I've known you all my life."

"So. Maybe I said something. Triggered your girlfriend. I'm sure it's no big deal. She probably ran off home."

"What the fuck, Harper?" I climb to my feet, already reachin' for my keys.

"She wanted to borrow my Audi," she slurs.

"Did you let her?"

"Come on, Scrappy. I told her no. We had words. Yadda, yadda, yadda. She's got my Audi."

"Where'd she go?"

"I'm sure she's heading home. It's just—" There's a long pause, and I'm about to lose my shit. "Wall called Grinder. He's at her place. He says Crista's not there."

"Where would she go?" Anger and alarm war inside me. It's only ten years of hiding all my shit from prying eyes that keeps my voice level.

"That's the thing. She wouldn't go anywhere else. It's been long enough. She should be at Pig Iron's or her place if that's where she was going. I'd go looking myself, but...I'm more than a little drunk. And like, we're not each other's favorite people right now."

"You're a fucking bitch, Harper, you know that."

"I do, Scrappy." She heaves a sigh. "I got a bad feeling about this."

And that's it. I'm already out the door. A pair of boots fall into step behind me. Forty and I are on the road, racing toward Gracy Avenue, and I'm searching for a silver Audi or a girl in a light green hoodie as I fight the pictures in my head, the blood and piss on concrete, the whimpering moans, the wet heat on my chest, and the smell of copper and gasoline.

16

CRISTA

I'm ten feet from Donny Mulvaney, his back to me as he pumps gas in an old Buick, my hand on the gun in my pocket, when two bikes come roaring down Gracy Avenue. Mulvaney startles, his gaze flying to the street, and then he bolts like a rabbit around the gas station.

I run after him without thinking, pumping my arms, around the back to where the employees park in a busted up, weed-choked lot surrounded by an old privacy fence. Mulvaney's scrambling at his car door with his keys when I catch up, gasping for air.

I skid to a halt a dozen feet away, and I pull out the Beretta. I cock it. You can hardly hear the click over my wheezing, but Mulvaney must see me from the corner of his eye. He freezes. His keys drop to the ground.

He raises his hands, slow, like he's done this before, but he doesn't even turn around to face me. His skinny back is heaving. Up close, he's shorter than I thought. Thinner. There are scabs on his elbows.

My clench my hands tighter on the gun to stop the shaking.

And then Scrap and Forty roar into the lot. They leap off their bikes, come running. Forty's on his phone.

"Send some prospects down Gracy," he's shouting. "Have 'em drag. Run lights. Whatever. Draw the cops to the west side. We're behind the gas station." There's a pause. "Guess there's been a change of plans, boss man."

Then they careen to a stop behind me on either side.

The Beretta only weighs seventeen ounces. That's one of the reasons we bought it. So I could hold it level for as long as I needed to, even with my weak upper arms. It hasn't even been a minute. Why are my hands shaking so bad? I'm not so weak as this.

I cup my palm, steady my aim. Mulvaney's shoulders slump, and he lowers his hands on the roof of his car. It's a piece of shit red Tercel. They don't even make them anymore.

What am I doing?

Am I going to shoot him?

I could shoot him. I could make him turn around, and I could shoot him in the gut. He could grab his stomach and try to hold himself together, but come up with palms slick with blood.

I should shoot him.

It's so quiet back here. Forty's hung up the phone, so no one's speaking now. The traffic on Gracy Avenue is muted. I can hear the gravel shift under Scrap's boots. I don't look at him, but I can feel him behind me, tall and calm.

Hot tears are dripping from my chin. When did they start again?

"I'm gonna touch your hand, Crista, okay? I ain't gonna take the gun." Scrap's voice is low. Unhurried. And then his arms reach around me, and his hands cups mine, helping me hold the gun steady. His chest is firm against my back. When he speaks, it's over my head.

"So what are we doin' here, baby?"

"I— I—"

"You know this guy?" His head is lowered so he can speak into my ear, his breath hot on my neck. My palms are so sweaty, my grip slips, but his forearms are bracing me, his fingers keeping mine on the trigger. "Who is he to you?"

When I tell, it has the bitter flavor of a confession. "He was there." My voice breaks, a jagged cry escaping. "He was there, too. With Inch Johnson."

Behind us, Forty growls. Then, suddenly, there's the roar of engines, and the crunch of tires and boots hitting the gravel—four or five men join us—but no one speaks.

Mulvaney's chest shudders. "If you let me go, I won't say shit to no one," he cries over his shoulder.

"Shut the fuck up." That's Heavy, his voice booming from behind.

I start to sob, a low keening, and Scrap wraps me closer, an arm lowering to wind around my waist, cradling me to him. "What do you wanna to do here, baby? It's your call."

I don't know. I want it to be over. I want it to have never happened. I want to be the kind of person who can kill a man. I want that so fucking bad.

I shake my head, and my mouth opens, but no words will come.

"You can let go," he says.

"I can't," I cry, but my grip is weak, all of me is weak, and Scrap's the only thing holding me up. "I can't." This time, it's a ragged whimper.

"Baby, look around. You're not alone." And I do. To my left, Forty and Wall have their weapons raised. To my right,

Heavy and Dizzy. "You can let go. I got you. We got you. Let's go home, baby. Frances is waiting on us."

He says it so quiet, there's no way anyone but me can hear what I do in his voice. The fear. The sheer terror I've only heard a few times before. In my father's voice when he cradled my head in that garage. In Mom's voice when she screamed at the doctors that they were *not* going to let me die.

I didn't get it. Not until this very second. I didn't understand that Scrap Allenbach needs me. That even though I can't begin to understand why, he loves me.

"It's going to be okay," I tell him.

"All right, baby," he says, and I know in my bones, it's not a gun I hold in my hands. It's his heart.

I let go, let Scrap take the gun. "Okay. It's over. We can go. I'm parked across the road."

There's a flurry of motion as four men rush past us, and a shout from Mulvaney that's muffled almost as soon as it starts. The last I see of him, Forty's throwing his limp body into the back of his Jeep, blood staining his white T-shirt.

Scrap takes me by the hand and leads me back around the building. There's a good dozen brothers converged out front, but no customers. Cue is having a word with a kid who looks like the manager.

We go back to the Audi, and Scrap opens the passenger door. I slide in. He loops around to the driver's side door and slides in, pushing the seat all the way back. He stretches his legs as far forward as they can go, and rests his arm on the back of the seat.

We sit there together, facing the gas station while cars drive past on Gracy Avenue and slow to gawk at all the bikes parked out front. Not soon after, I realize I'm sobbing, and then after a while, the sobs turn to hiccups. Scrap waits next to me, quiet and still, filling the car with the smell of leather and sweat.

After what feels like a very long time, after all the bikes have pulled off, and a red Tercel with Wall behind the wheel pulls out from behind the gas station, Scrap clears his throat.

"You remember at the garage? When you asked me to tell you what I remember from back then?" he says.

"Yeah." I sniff and wipe my face with my sleeve.

"I remember being in love with you." He looks at me, his blue eyes overflowing. "I was in love with you, Crista Holt. I *am* in love with you, but I been in love with you forever. From all the way back when you'd sit out under Twitch and Shirl's tree, readin' books, and I'd wash my bike in the yard, tryin' to see what you were reading. Like maybe if I read what you read, I'd know how to talk to you. Fuckin' *The Odyssey. A Tale of Two Cities.*"

"That was freshman year." My voice comes out ragged.

"Yeah, I know. You were too damn young. I felt like such a sick fuck. If Pig Iron had known what was goin' through my mind, he would've killed me." Scrap chuckles, like the memory isn't a bad one. "Back then, I had the notion that somehow Dad and Ma had talked to God when they saw Him. Told Him he needed to make up somehow for all the shit, and then there you were."

He shrugs, and then he inhales, deep.

"After we found you that day, they'd only let Pig Iron ride in the ambulance. We all followed behind. You were in surgery for hours. I sat in that waiting room, and I prayed so fucking hard. You weren't a crush, Crista Holt. I been in love with you since I knew what love was."

I didn't think there were more tears in me, but they're back, slowly rolling down my cheeks, my neck.

"It was the second night. Pig Iron came out. A few of us were in the waiting room. Most of the brothers were out lookin' for Inch. Pig Iron said the doctor told him you wasn't gonna make it. That if any of us wanted to say our goodbyes, we best do it."

I didn't know this part. I know the doctors said I wouldn't make it, but goodbyes? No one had ever mentioned it.

"Bullet and I went back to where they had you in this little cubicle. There was a huge machine next to your bed, a nurse workin' it, a mask covering your face. I don't think you were breathin' on your own. Deb was standin' beside you, holdin' your hand. She saw us, and she lost her shit."

Mom has told me this part. A few times, when things got really hard, especially when I started leaning too heavy on the meds, Deb would lose her shit on me and scream, "I didn't let those fuckers at Petty's Mill General give up on you, and I ain't letting you give up on yourself."

"Deb told us we could shove our last words up our asses." Scrap chuckles. "She told us to go be useful and kill the motherfucker who did this to her daughter."

He pauses a moment and his face goes somber again. "I knew you were gonna die. There was so much blood, baby. I *knew* no one could make it. I went crazy."

He reaches out and brushes a finger down my cheek, his blue eyes searing mine. "I thought you were gonna die, and if you were gone, nothing fucking mattered. So I went and killed Inch Johnson, and you lived. 'Cause I gave up hope, I left you alone for ten years when it was my job to be there for you. How am I gonna forgive myself for that? How could I ask you to forgive me for that?"

His pain is raw and real in his voice. It hurts worse than my own, and I want so badly to take it from him. To carry it for him. But I can't.

"I love you," I say instead.

But it's like a dam broke, and he keeps talking, way more words than I ever heard him string together before.

"Everyone wondered how I kept goin' inside. After I got jumped, and I sent you away 'cause I couldn't bear you seein' that shit after what you went through, the brothers were always watchin' me like I was gonna lose it. But they didn't understand."

"What? What didn't they understand?" My hand reaches for his face, and he nuzzles his cheek into my palm.

"Prison wasn't hell. Those days when I thought you were gonna die? That was hell. But you lived. So I could live. Through anything." His takes my hand and drops a kiss in the center.

I lean up and brush his lips with mine. "I love you," I say again.

"Don't ever fuckin' try to shoot a man on Main Street again."

"It's Gracy Avenue. And I was out the back."

"Don't be a smartass and buckle your seatbelt. We're goin' home."

Scrap puts the truck into gear, but before we pull out of the parking lot, Boom and Wash come flying down the street, whooping into the wind, all four of Petty's Mills cop cars giving chase at full speed, sirens blaring.

"Harper's gonna have a busy night," I say.

"Serves her right." Scrap turns the opposite direction of the chase and heads south.

I sink back in the seat, and I let Scrap's strength and calm soothe me as I breathe it in.

I haven't loved Scrap since I knew what love was. I don't know when I started to love him, but I know I'll never stop. He's sitting next to me, and yet, it doesn't feel like that.

It feels like I've finally found my heart, and to my surprise, it's been living outside my body, beating strong and steady this whole time. Whatever parts of me are missing—and will always be missing—don't hurt so bad 'cause Scrap Allenbach is taking me home. I'm not alone, and neither is he, and for once, everything is right with the world.

THE WALK up the mountain almost kills me.

When Heavy pulled me aside and asked me if I wanted to see things through to the end, I didn't think twice. I said yes. It takes about two miles straight up through the bush before I start thinking closure is over-fuckin'-rated.

Forty and Dad are carrying game bags slung over their shoulders containing the remains of Donny Mulvaney. When we start up the barely-there trail, Dad hands me a sapling in a burlap sack to hump up to the dump site. About fifteen minutes in, when I stumble over a fallen log, Scrap takes the sapling off my hands. I feel guilty 'cause he's outfitted with camping shit, too, but I can't lie. I'm worried I won't make it all the way to the top.

I'm not used to the outdoors. I'm not used to walking for more than a few minutes. The thing about a life with perimeters is you can't go too far in any direction. In retrospect, maybe the direction I should've gone first when I decided to bust out of my cage wasn't straight vertical.

I'm puffing and wheezing after an hour, and an hour after that, Dad and Forty stop waiting for me to catch up.

Scrap stays with me, patient as always. He hardly breaks a sweat.

About three hours in, we take a break. There's a flat rock about waist height, cut at an incline, and I basically collapse on it, arms flung wide. Scrap has to nudge my arm over to make room to sit.

"How you holdin' up?" He brings his knees to his chest and stares down the mountain. I bet it's a hell of a view, but I can't bring myself to sit back up, so I stare at the impossibly clear, blue sky, framed by the slow sweeping tops of tall pines. A hawk is circling so high up he winks in and out of view. It's like the world is so big my eyes don't know how to see it all.

"I'll make it," I say. Scrap passes me a canteen. We lapse into silence.

After a while, I turn my head away from the sky to look at him. His face is calm, like always, but there's something in his eyes. A reverence. He's gazing down at me. A half-smile tugs at his lips.

"Pretty, ain't it?" he says.

I nod.

"Best keep going." He stands, and offers me a hand. It takes me considerably longer to haul my ass up, but I do. The rest of the hike passes quickly.

When we get to a clearing with three newly planted trees, we come on Forty with a shovel, knee deep in a hole.

"Feels like I was just here," he jokes.

"Those the Rebel Raiders that went after Fay-Lee and Roosevelt at Twiggy's?" Scrap asks, waving at the three little saplings.

Forty nods. "And Ike Kobald. We should water them since we're up here. A little help?"

Scrap peels his shirt off, grabs another shovel, and gets to work. Dad spells him after a while, and I'm glad no one asks me. It takes me most of the time they spend digging to catch my breath.

Scrap told me on the way here how it would go. Steel Bones has a tradition of burying its bodies up in the Shady Mountains, planting a tree on top of the burned corpse. It's poetic, but practical, too. Wildlife doesn't dig up bones covered by trees.

As the men finish the hole and wander off to store the shovels wherever they keep them, I'm left alone with the game bags. It's strange, knowing it's over. And that it doesn't change much of anything.

This is the farthest I've come since that day when I was sixteen, but Donny Mulvaney being dead doesn't really have much to do with it. If I trace my steps back, farther and farther and farther, I started this hike long before he disappeared into Forty's Jeep that day at the gas station and never showed up for work again.

Before I decided to go dancing with Fay-Lee and Nevaeh. Before I let Scrap ride me home.

If I let myself think about it—and I never do, but maybe I will this once—this hike began at Petty's Mill General Hospital. They'd taken out my catheter, and I had to pee. For once, Mom wasn't there. I think she was getting a Coke from the machine. I was alone. I used the remote to raise the back of the bed all the way, and then I used my hands to maneuver my legs over the side. I couldn't use my stomach muscles at all at that point.

I wasn't thinking clearly. I was so doped up in those days. I think I kind of counted three in my head and then willed my abdominals to help me stand. There was a horrible, stabbing pain, and I sort of slid off the side of the bed onto the floor like I was made of rubber. I couldn't get up. I couldn't reach the remote to hit the help button. So for a few minutes, I laid on the nasty hospital floor, my cheek pressed to the cold tile.

It hurt, and I was scared, and I knew in a minute or ten the horror of what happened would rise up yet again, flapping and pecking at my mind like crows, but then? In that moment? I was so fucking happy. I was alive.

When Forty and Dad come back, they dump Mulvaney in the hole and light him up with gasoline. I stay back, next to Scrap.

For a second, I'm afraid the smell will send me over the edge, but I stay in control. It helps that Scrap's beside me. After the flames ebb, we say our goodbyes and head off on our own.

It was Scrap's idea to split from Dad and Forty on the way back down the mountain. He wants to take a detour to a place he used to go with his father when he was a kid. They used to hunt on this mountain, and this was a place they'd go to fly fish. Scrap says there's a pool, and a rapid that runs over an incline just steep enough that it could be called a waterfall. He talks about it like Narnia or something, so I said we could go. In for a penny, in for a pound, right?

As we take off down the mountain, I kind of wish I hadn't. It's like now that the weight of what we needed to do is gone, all my aches and pains have decided to pipe up. Scrap has perked up since the grisly shit is behind us, and he's stoked there's only a three-hour hike left before we get to his camping spot.

I'm not gonna make it. I'm faking like I have to pee all the time so I can sit for a minute and catch my breath. My boots have rubbed my heels raw, and I reek of smoke and sweat. I'm trying so hard to keep up with Scrap's long legs, my jeans have chafed the inside of my thighs bright red.

"You good back there?" Scrap's waiting for me at a treefall. He's hauling all our gear. I should feel guilty, but all I feel is cranky. Now that the catharsis is over, this royally sucks.

"How much further?"

He checks his GPS. "It's real close."

Close is relative. I'm almost in tears by the time I hear the water, and Scrap lifts his arms wide and spins in a slow circle, grinning with both sides of his mouth cocked up.

"What do you think? Ain't it gorgeous."

I sink to my butt on a dirt patch next to the river. I guess you'd call it a river. It's narrow, but deep, and if you're generous, there is a waterfall spilling over into a blue pool. There are smooth, round rocks on the banks, and a few yards past where we've stopped, the river bends out of sight among the huge pines.

Okay, it *is* beautiful. "It'll do, I guess."

Scrap drops a kiss on the top of my head. "You stay there. I'm gonna set up camp."

No problem with that. I couldn't get off my ass if I wanted to. Since I've taken the pressure off my feet, they're pulsing and swollen.

Scrap bustles around, laying out a tarp, pitching the tent. I've never seen him like this. He's like a kid. He builds a fire, but he doesn't light it yet. It's getting to be late in the afternoon, and a breeze is picking up, but it's not cool.

I like just watching him work. He's got his shirt off, and you can see his muscles flex as he moves. He does each chore like he's been doing it for years, navigates the stones and the sticks like he's never been locked away.

My heart aches, and an unbearable weight settles on my shoulders.

"I'm so sorry."

Scrap looks up from where he's squatting, tying back a flap on the tent, a question in his eyes.

"I'm so sorry." My voice breaks.

He takes a minute to reply. "I am, too," he finally says. "But I'm other shit as well, you know?"

I do. I am, too. Relieved and angry and full of hope for the first time in forever. And in love. So fucking in love. And when our eyes meet across the camp, I see all of that and more reflected in his eyes.

Finally, when he's done fussing with all the stakes and ties and gear, he makes his way over to me. "Feet hurt?"

"Yup."

He sinks down and pulls my boots onto his lap. "Hey. What are you doing?" After this hike, my feet are gonna reek.

"We've got enough time to go swimming before it gets dark if we do it now."

Nope. No way. "Who said anything about swimming?"

He waves his hand around. "I brought you to a waterfall, woman. What did you think we were gonna do?"

"I'm not prepared for this." Not in any way. It's broad daylight. I'm wearing jeans.

"I know." He drops a kiss on my nose, and then he applies himself to unlacing my boots. As he tugs them off, I can't help but sigh, loud and long.

"That feel good?"

"Yeah." And then he peels off my socks. I try to pull my feet away, but he's got them good. He draws them closer and checks the blisters on my heel.

"No broken skin. That's good."

And then he moves his hands to the zipper of my hoodie. "This has to come off, too."

My heart leaps in my chest. I brace myself for panic, but it doesn't come. Not quite. Instead there's a quickening in my pulse, a jittery dance in my belly.

Am I going to do this?

I'm out in the wilderness for the first time since I was a kid, and there's nothing around for miles but owls and foxes. Scrap swears there's no bears. There are no people, no eyes but his. And his eyes on me don't hurt.

He unzips my hoodie and eases it off my shoulders. "I'll stick this in the tent for later."

He hops to his feet with admirable lack of groaning, and then he's back, offering me his hand. I take it, and he pulls me up.

"This next." He draws my arms into the air, and looks me a question. I leave them raised.

He takes the hem of my tank top and gently peels it over my head. I can't look down, so I watch him instead. His eyes rake down from my white bra to my bare, white belly. I wait for my lungs to seize, for the noise in my mind to swell to a cacophony.

Maybe this place is Narnia. There's some magic here 'cause I stay in the moment. The sun on my shoulders. The birds calling to each other way high overhead. I glance down.

The big scar is an angry, reddish pink diagonal from my breast down into the waistband of the jeans. I've got a dozen others, too, silvery white, some puckered. Fucked up constellations. The best you can say about them is most don't hurt anymore unless I turn a certain way.

The big scar is the eye-catcher, though. Even I look at it

and wonder that a human's body could knit back together from something like that.

Scrap keeps staring, and now I'm turning red, a flush blossoming across my chest.

"You done?" My voice is sharp. I raise my chin.

"Nope." He drops his gaze, and then he's unbuttoning my jeans. He takes a moment to unbutton and shuck his own, so now he's standing naked in front of me, his cock bobbing straight up in the air. He rolls down my jeans, panties and all.

"Step out."

I step out of my jeans 'cause I don't know what else to do.

Scrap grabs both my hands, and he lifts my arms to the side. Then he smiles his half-smile and bends to kiss me, long and sweet.

"You don't have to act like it isn't hideous." I wrap my arms around my middle.

"I don't have to act like it is, either." He kisses me on the nose. "Let's go swimming, baby. We're wasting the light."

Then he grabs my hand and guides me, naked and jiggling, trying desperately to cover my most jiggly bits and failing, into the pool under Pennsylvania's saddest little waterfall.

The water is cold, and holy Lord, it feels amazing on my feet. Scrap sighs as he traipses to the middle and sinks in to his chest.

"Come on, babe. It's waist deep here."

"It's cold."

"It's warmer out here."

"Bullshit."

"Come find out." He laughs and splashes me, gets my hair wet, and I can't let that stand. I shriek and splash him back, and then I'm in the middle of the river, too, and we're twisted together, the water up to our chests, and we're float-ing, intertwined, his legs hot against mine, my skin slick against his.

He takes my hand and guides it under the water.

"Feel this." He juts into my palm, hard, thick and hot. My heart speeds up.

We haven't gone this far since the face stomping incident.

He must see the worry cross my face. "Chill out, baby. I ain't gonna fall for a sneak attack more than once."

"You didn't just—" I sputter, and he takes my hand and moves it up and down his shaft, and his breathing hitches. His eyes are bright, and there's a hunger in them that rouses warm, fizzy bubbles in my stomach.

"Come on."

He leads me back to the bank, the water sluicing off of his carved chest. Before I can cover myself, he's guiding me across the smooth rocks, to the tent he's pitched.

"Check it out."

He helps me down, following quickly, and it's all going so fast I don't think about the scars and the angles and the jiggling. He's inflated an air mattress, and there's a sleeping bag unzipped to double size across it. He pats the ground, but he doesn't have to. It's so soft and comfy, I lay flat, stretching out all the aches and pains, and he lays down beside me, smiling, toying with my hair.

"You like the air mattress?"

"I love it."

"You love your old man." He strokes down between my breasts, glancing over my belly, and plays with the curls between my legs.

"I do." My tired, clean body has turned my mind mellow and malleable.

"Open up for me, baby." I bend my knees, and his rough fingers slip between my folds. He keeps his eyes on my face, kissing me, sliding his tongue along mine, tasting and teasing, and then he backs up, meets my gaze, smiles.

My pussy begins to throb, especially around the nub he teases, circles, then neglects while he runs his hands down my thighs and up to my aching breasts. He's touching me all over, not lingering anywhere long, and every stroke eases an ache or stokes a longing.

My hands get antsy, and I touch him, too. His hard chest, the hair curled and damp from the river. His cock, even harder now and hotter, dripping precum from the tip. His breath picks up, and his blue eyes swirl in the deepening shadows. Outside, the cricket chorus swells and recedes.

My body is sore and alive. My hips begin to rock of their own accord.

"Like that, eh?" Scrap keeps the tempo that makes me squirm, and he starts to rise above me. I tense. Without missing a beat, he lowers himself back to the mattress, and rolls me on top of him. His cock nudges at my pussy, and I start rocking again while he grins up at me, as happy as I've ever seen him.

It's coming. My belly is coiling tighter and tighter, and if I were alone in my bed, I'd know how to chase this down, use my fingers to ease this ache.

"Scrap," I whine because I want it. He urges me to bend closer, sips at my lips, nips at my neck, and glides his hot cock through my folds, up and back.

"I know, baby. We'll get there. We ain't in no rush, are we?"

I guess not.

He notches his cock in my entrance, and this time, I'm drenched for him. He guides me down and thrusts inside me in one smooth motion, pauses a second to read my face, but I'm okay, and it's perfect. He smiles, and then moves, and it's like he's stoking the fire higher. He groans in my ear. "You're so fucking soft. So perfect."

He twines our fingers, bringing our hands to rest on his chest right above his heart,, and he watches me with the corner of his mouth quirked up as he rocks deeper and deeper, steady, and now I'm bucking, grinding down, searching after more, and he lets my hands go so he can sneak his calloused fingers back between us to find the little bud that's pulsing and needy for him.

He circles and circles, thrusting into me with his hot cock and then withdrawing to the tip, only to urge me to sink down on him, and it's too much, and not enough, and I'm whimpering, my fingers warring with his to get at my clit, and then I'm there, exploding, waves bursting outward through my whole body while my belly quivers and my thighs shake.

I scream, and Scrap laughs softly, so happy, and then he shouts as he cums hot inside me.

"That was—That was—" I'm entirely out of breath.

"Us. Together. The way we're always gonna be for the rest of our lives."

"Wet and stinky and loud in a tent?"

"Yup." Scrap slaps my ass. "Exactly."

"Can we bring Frances next time?"

"Sure thing. You'll need to carry him though. You know he ain't about to hike up no mountain."

I sigh. "Well, there goes that plan."

Scrap's quiet a moment. "Shit, woman. You know I'll carry your dog."

"Yeah?" I wriggle to kiss him, to get even closer.

"Yeah."

A while later, I drift off, cocooned in warmth and the smell of pine, lulled to sleep by water rushing over rock and Scrap Allenbach's breath beneath me. The world outside the tent feels beautiful, boundless, and alive. And so do I.

THE STEEL BONES saga continues in Plum.

A NOTE FROM THE AUTHOR

Will Ernestine ever take Grinder back?
Will Creech ever find someone to love him?
Who was Boots' 'California Girl,' and where did she go?

I have no idea!
But you will be the first to know if you sign up for my
newsletter at www.catecwells.com!

You'll get a FREE novella, too!

ABOUT THE AUTHOR

Cate C. Wells indulges herself in everything from motorcycle club to small town to mafia to paranormal romance. Whatever the subgenera, readers can expect character-driven stories that are raw, real, and emotionally satisfying romance. She's into messy love, flaws, long roads to redemption, grace, and happily ever after, in books and in life.

Along with stories, she's collected a husband and three children along the way. She lives in Baltimore when she's not exploring the world with the family.

I love to connect with readers! Meet me in The Cate C. Wells Reader Group on Facebook.

Facebook: @catecwells
Twitter: @CateCWells1
Bookbub: @catecwells

Printed in Great Britain
by Amazon

21532402R10120